All About Town

Also by the Author
The Clock Tower (2017)

All About Town

Michael McGrath

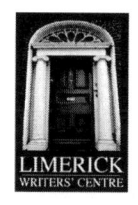

Limerick Writers' Centre
Publishing

Limerick - Ireland

Copyright © Michael McGrath 2019

First published in Ireland by The Limerick Writers' Centre
12 Barrington Street Limerick, Ireland

www.limerickwriterscentre.com
www.facebook.com/limerickwriterscentre

All rights reserved

1 3 5 7 9 10 8 6 4 2

No part of this publication may be reproduced or transmitted in any form or by any means, electronic or mechanical without permission in writing from the publisher, except by a reviewer who may quote brief passages in a review.

Book Design: Lotte Bender.
Cover Image: Chris McMorrow (www.chrismcmorrow.net)
Managing Editor: Dominic Taylor

ISBN 978-1-9160653-3-8

ACIP catalogue number for this publication is available from The British Library

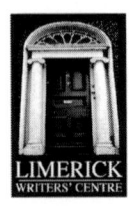

For Cillian

Contents

Acknowledgements — ix

The Glass and the Globe — 11

The Envelope — 21

A Visitor — 29

Minerva and the Star — 36

Jenny — 38

April 1919 — 43

Spanish Point — 46

A Study in F — 51

Circles of the Moon — 64

Someone I loved in Ireland — 67

About the Author — *70*

About the Limerick Writers' Centre — *71*

Acknowledgements

I'd like to thank my mother, father, children and all of my family for their continued support. A special thank you to Dominic Taylor, Michael Griffin, Mr. McHugh and Chris McMorrow. Thanks also to Dermot McCabe and all at the Abraxus writing group in Bray.

And to everyone who buys and reads my books. These first editions will be worth a lot of money someday you know…

The Glass and the Globe

Six months had passed since Eva's boots last trod along the damp streets of Limerick and little seemed to have changed in their absence. Grey-bellied clouds still hovered above rooftops in Zeppelin formations and the gutters gargled beneath fleet footsteps and umbrellas. All about town, busy figures hurried from one shelter to the next with few pausing to admire the city's wet vistas or the sheen from the stone flags of her pavements. "Indeed," Eva whispered as she brought a glass of Burgundy wine to her lips, "familiar."

The young woman had wandered through all her favourite shops for the first time in months, gleeful for the novelty they now came to possess. It seemed only fitting then, that she should round off the evening with a bite and a drink in her favourite restaurant in the city.

The Belle Italia not only served marinated pasta and delicate wines, it had offered sanctuary in a turbulent world throughout the short span of Eva's adult life. Escaping from the earth, the girl would disappear down its rabbit hole and discover herself wrapped in blankets of melodies, pastries and dark furnishings.

"Oh, how wonderful," she whispered again – louder this time – and placed the heel of her palm to her mouth. She should probably slow down. It was unusual for her to drink so quickly but these were unusual circumstances. Granny O'Shea had passed away very quickly in the end. It seemed an oddity for the living that prolonged illnesses did nothing to mask the shock of death. Dementia had taken away the granny they had known many years ago before cancer returned to collect the shell that remained.

Eva watched the rim of her wine glass distort behind the sudden rush of water to her eyes. Granny O'Shea had always been very good to her when she had known herself to be an awkward child. The sweets that were hidden in the cupboard under the sink were always their little secret; the fairy-tales she would read to her as she sat upon her lap by the old open fire were the highlight of many weekends; and even in adulthood, Eva could never leave her grandmother's company without receiving a warm embrace and a kind word in her ear.

In a peculiar way, Granny O'Shea had offered a parting gift with her passing: she had granted Eva her first trip home since her move to Melbourne six months previously. And for that, Eva whispered – this time in her head – she should thank her grandmother dearly.

"Everything okay?" asked the Eastern European voice of a slim waitress who stood patiently over Eva's table. The evening was moving steadily along, and the city's streetlamps had begun to cast long shadows over the pavements and puddles outside her window. It was surely too dreary to venture back outside for the moment. Yes, best to let the sharp end of the showers pass.

"I'll have one more glass of the Burgundy, if you don't mind?"

It was true that Eva had felt out of sorts since the warm air surrounded her face as she disembarked her plane and stood on the hot tarmac of Melbourne. Any grand adventure would always be marked by adversity and money was scarce in the hospitality sector. It would all work out fine, her friends at home and abroad reassured her.

Yet, as she tumbled anxiously in her Australian sleep, Eva acknowledged the pangs of hunger and home drumming relentlessly against the sides of her stomach. She scratched and tossed about the bed she had made for herself and wondered in awe towards the strange constellations of the southern hemisphere. Before dawn, she would draw herself upright against the headboard and pen the latest entry on the soft paper of her travel diary – fearful of where honesty may guide her hand.

What would Cian make of it all? He had wished her nothing but happiness when he kissed her in Shannon, and she believed him. He didn't want the drama of going to the airport, but she had insisted. A group of her friends would need to see her off and Cian was a dear childhood friend long before he became something else.

The young waitress had returned and carefully placed a glass of red wine on the floral tablecloth. Eva met her smile with her own. The rain had not relented, and its cool rivers snaked in abstract patterns down the surface of the window. She scanned the floating faces beneath the restaurant's dim lights and looked once more toward her fresh glass of Burgundy. The airport had hurt him.

****

South's Bar was rarely quiet on a Tuesday evening which was due in part to the multitude of midweek sporting events that played out on its numerous screens. It was surprising then, to Cian, that the long and spacious bar should only be populated by a mild sprinkling of patrons after six o'clock. He also noted that the classical décor which included glass panels and various brass fittings could be admired all the more without the regular drinker leaning against them. For the first time in many months, the young man began to soak in the pleasing aesthetic of his usual drinking haunt: the chandeliers twinkling above his glassy eyes and the occasional potted plant provided a shock of green to the otherwise light timbered furnishings of a pleasantly antiquated bar.

Behind the counter, old Jim was busily polishing the insides of a whiskey glass and confirming the bad news that Cian had now come to suspect: "No Champions League matches on tonight, I'm afraid."

"Ah Jesus," Cian muttered into the cream of his pint of stout. It was a fright when football failed to provide him with adequate cover for midweek drinks. Instead of falling into a liminal trance in front of colourful screens, he'd now be looking at polished shelves of bottles and the comings and goings of old Jim. He could go home of course.

"I might have a Jameson with that, Jim."

The barman was already standing near the whiskey optics, knowing the young man's habits, and nodded in acknowledgment. Old Jim had first noticed Cian slipping into the bar more frequently after Christmas. Now they had travelled round to late September once more, and the young fella seemed to occupy his usual spot at the bend of the counter more nights than not. He was always on his own.

Cian slid four coins across the counter to cover his whiskey and brought a phone out of his trouser pocket to check the football fixtures. Surely there was a cup game on? It was a highly unusual situation and he began to feel vexed at the suited men who created football fixtures for allowing this black hole in his entertainment to fester.

It was no use. Stepping off the high stool, he ambled with a gait beyond his years to the bar's entrance, collected a copy of yesterday's *Limerick Post*, and brought it back to his perch for review. He might see someone he knew in the social sections and it was better than looking at old Jim.

The newspaper's pages were jumbled, and most were tattered and stained with unknown foods. As he flattened the front section along the countertop, Cian's eyes were drawn to a local politician who was pictured standing in front of a derelict house. The man's round face was flushed, and his features had contracted to a fiery scowl. Something to do with the housing crisis, Cian postulated over his whiskey glass and began to grasp at various threads in his mind – any one of which could unravel his solution to Ireland's lack of affordable accommodation.

It was little wonder that Eva had wanted to leave the damp soil behind her and feel the sun heating her bones in Melbourne. She needed to travel before she settled down and he knew that was reasonable. Their young relationship had burned brightly but should be no barrier to her dreams.

Yet in his distorted image upon the bar's brass fittings, a sorrow hung from the edges of his tired features. The six months since Eva's departure furrowed lines of sleepless nights beneath his eyes. She had asked him to go with her, but he'd strongly resisted the idea of leaving his job and family – even leaving Limerick itself behind for three years. And now, without the warmth of her words and skin next to his, the city seemed a less familiar place. And old Jim and the old bar mocked him.

****

The autumn sun was sinking beneath the uneven rooftops of Thomas Street, streaking its orange face against the grey canvas of the sky. A group of rainclouds had separated respectfully to mourn the passing of another day and darkness chased long shadows from the pavements.

The Belle Italia had begun to slip into the bustling night period and the flow of families and couples increased with the dimming of its lights. Eva wondered how long she had been sitting alone at her table and began to feel guilty at occupying a window seat now that the restaurant's custom was starting to peak. The rise in the volume of both people and sound had also distorted the earlier ambience that she had so merrily enjoyed. With each passing hour, more raised voices and sizzling plates echoed from dark corners and lively tables. She knew it would soon be time to leave them all to their evenings.

It was a blessing that she and Cian had never eaten here. That no memories of him hung behind the shadows on the seats or glowed beneath the lamps. This oasis of her teens had remained unspoiled into adulthood and she could return to consume its comforts in quiet solitude.

She felt sure that Cian had dark corners of his own, but he never told her of them. He was odd in that way. Despite an outgoing nature, he would sometimes disappear for two or three days and refuse to speak about where he was. Eva surmised that their relationship was too fresh for her to assume the role of a nagging wife – nor would she have herself lowered to it. Yet she was instinctively curious as to where he wandered to for those discomforting spells.

While considering these memories, Eva sensed the mild guilt around her own sanctuary in the Belle Italia lift from her shoulders. "Fuck him," she giggled into her glass of Burgundy, "he doesn't have a monopoly on secrets."

Ah, Jesus. She was getting drunk now. And she felt sure the waitress had cast a sideways glance the last few times she had walked by her seat. The fourth glass seemed to have been poured right into her head, and the table swayed on the high seas of life.

It hadn't always been that way with Cian. She remembered when their childhood friendship slowly crossed the rubicon of affection and was replaced by the sparkling newness of a romantic relationship. It was natural and tender. The ease at which they felt in each other's arms was reassuring and the transition was almost seamless.

Sometimes he would arrive at her door unannounced and ask if she wanted to go for a walk and a coffee. It irked her slightly as she was usually dressed for an evening on the couch. Yet he always complimented what she was wearing and said that he understood why makeup was important to a girl, but for what it was worth, he preferred her without it. He would say that she was beautiful in any circumstance or any clothes and that he had always thought so. And when he told her this, he did so with a sincerity in his eyes that seemed to come from years of quiet admiration.

They would stroll hand in hand by the quays, passing the Treaty Stone and looking across the river to the medieval towers poking above a red bricked modernity on the old King's Island. The breeze was always fresh, and swans bobbed about in groups of twos and threes at the foot of the high stone walls. As she felt the warmth of his hand in her own, Eva would allow her gaze to fall upon their interlocking fingers: floating as they did above the scattered leaves and creaking timber decking beneath their feet. The comfort of those silences allowed them to reflect in each other's company. To live in their moments and nowhere else.

And when a conversation did begin, they had a lifetime of memories together to speak about. They knew each other's families, shared many of the same anecdotes, were never short of things to say.

Eva knew of a friend in that time who she had been unable to know since. And she missed him.

****

Some of the usual latecomers had started to drift into South's Bar from the cool autumn night and a circle of elderly gentlemen had formed around a table to play a game of forty-five. The conversations of those assembled at the bar were fluctuating between sports and politics, and Cian found himself biting his bottom lip when an opinion on either presented itself to his mind. Peace and hot whiskeys were now the order of the day, as his head was full of troubles and his belly was full of stout.

Carefully taking the hot glass which was rattling on a saucer from old Jim's trembling hands, Cian placed his drink upon the counter and stared admiringly at the paraphernalia which accompanied it. The teaspoon, napkin and two sachets of brown sugar provided him with a task that he would now need to consider, and that in itself was a welcome relief from his ruminations.

Pouring in the sugar, Cian noisily stirred it to a brown whirlpool and watched the grains swirl to a violent vortex before settling to the bottom of the glass. A sweet aroma of lemons and cloves drifted upward to his twitching nostrils and he inhaled them deep into his lungs. Swallowing a generous gulp, he enjoyed the heat slowly travelling down his chest, setting fires and creating light in previously damp and gloomy passages.

As he continued to drink, the numbness to his brain came quickly and was welcome. The idle chatter from the men nearby was becoming irksome and he longed to disappear into the wordless background music which floated between each sentence.

There was a time when he would rescue himself from the world by hiding in isolation along the banks of the Shannon near Killaloe. Here, he would submit himself to nature and pass his time near the foot of a fishing rod; reading and meditating with his toes dangling just above the surface of the lapping water. His small tent was hardy and weatherproof and could fit supplies for many days. Each morning he would take long walks into the trees of a countryside he wished he'd been fortunate enough to grow up in. And he was never lonely.

Eva would often ask where he was during those days, but he couldn't tell her. He wanted to keep something of himself from human knowledge. That only the natural world itself should be privy to his sanctuary; and he knew the trees and the animals were nothing if not apt at keeping a secret.

It was strange then, that contentment in his early adult life had only visited itself upon him through magnetic opposites: isolation by the river and the company of Eva. Only six months ago he had both – and now he had neither. Various pubs had slowly replaced the river and a space in his heart had replaced Eva.

He remembered walking along the quays past the Treaty Stone on those warm September evenings last autumn. Her hand was hot in his, but he didn't want to let it go. The wide footpaths and first fallen leaves lay as though posing for postcards under their feet and he felt his breath quickening as they approached the grey stone pillars of Sarsfield Bridge. They stopped to admire the red hues of the failing sun upon the river and he was taken back by a similar glow radiating from her eyes. He had never known – never imagined, such a tender and beautiful thing. Cradling her face gently with both hands, he kissed her lips and felt their warmth press against his. A gust from the river blew her blonde hair all about his hands, brushing off his skin and trailing in scattered loops through the air.

The moment was forever.

****

Eva sipped a second glass of water and scrolled through her phone for the taxi app. She had switched to water over an hour ago and was already feeling the edges of a hangover tickling the sides of her forehead. The time spent at the table by herself was now reaching four hours and oncoming sobriety was accompanied by a degree of self-consciousness. Yet going home drunk to her parents was such a non-runner that the judgement of strangers seemed a small price to pay. And so, keying in her location, she watched the loading screen's animation revolve until her taxi request was accepted: her car would arrive in nine minutes and be driven by a man named Paul Roche – a middle-aged sort with glasses who didn't seem to like posing for photographs.

The young waitress had fetched the bill and left it along with a small plate on the edge of the table. Eva read the slip of paper with a sprinkle of apprehension and realised she was now sober enough to be taken aback. The evening had been totted up to sixty-eight euros and forty cents – more than two-thirds of which was alcohol based. Good Lord. More than a hundred Australian dollars with nothing to show for it beyond a queasy stomach and a dizzy head. And she still had to pay for a cab home.

Still, it was a rare treat, she reassured herself, and it wasn't as if she could do it next week. No, next week she would be folding towels and cleaning bedrooms in Melbourne – gazing through the glass of the hotel's windows and knowing the value of a penny. She would return to her bedsit to write her travel diaries and once again stare out at the southern constellations. And she would be far away from the raindrops and puddles of Limerick.

Somewhere within the blurred lights of the city, Cian was experiencing his life without her. He was carrying on as people must do, and she hated herself for wondering how often he thought about her. How cruel a person she must be for wanting him to miss her. To desire that for someone whom she had left behind.

She could have told him that she was back for the few days. It wouldn't have been difficult to find a few hours to meet him if he had wanted that. Now he would know she was home through friends, and he would hate her for not getting in touch. Or maybe he would understand that she did it to spare them both another goodbye.

Her cab was due in less than two minutes. Leaving a generous tip for the waitress, Eva slid a faux leather jacket around her shoulders and steadied herself on her feet – thankful for the absence of heels. The restaurant had quietened off considerably and the small team of waiting staff was wiping down tables and bringing plates and cutlery to the kitchen.

It had been a pleasant evening and Eva had enjoyed the ambience of the fine dining experience just as she had done when she was a resident of the city. She would do it again next year and she knew she would do so on her own. Cian had moved on. She could see his happy eyes, boyish and gleeful as they were when he first held her hand – undampened by another farewell. Understanding that detail alone made the bill and the tip a small sum to pay from her purse.

The thin front door of the restaurant rattled in its frame as she placed her hand on the steel handle – conditions outside had worsened. Glancing once more to the dark furnishings as a forest creature would to the safety of its warren, Eva pushed the glass door and stepped out into the rain.

****

Last orders were being taken in South's Bar and the small groupings of patrons dutifully raised their fingers to gain old Jim's attention. The barman seemed more jaded than usual tonight, Cian surmised, the relative quietness of his shift ensuring he had difficulty putting down the time. Every speck of dust on the glasses and shelves had certainly been vanquished, and the young man found himself admiring the old timer's industry.

For his part, Cian ordered a single Jameson – neat. Work at the shop would be hectic tomorrow and he needed to be on his way.

Old Jim loudly hit the whiskey glass on the countertop and slid away a final twenty euro note which Cian had been hoping not to break tonight. Events in his head had put paid to that aspiration. Raising the small glass from the counter, the young man swallowed it in two unseemly attempts; wiping his mouth with the back of his shirt sleeve.

Old Jim returned with his change and Cian thanked him while sliding from his stool. The barman narrowed his eyes. "Have you any umbrella, young fella? Tis coming down in buckets again outside."

"Era, there's no fear of me at all, Jim – I've only a short stroll home."

Old Jim seemed unconvinced but understood the futility of arguing with Cian once he had given a few hours on the high stool. There were no umbrellas behind the bar, and he knew the young man wouldn't accept a taxi. "Well mind yourself, won't ya?" he conceded.

"I will, Jim. I'll be home in five minutes."

Saluting the people of the bar who he had barely spoken to all night, Cian walked slowly and deliberately to the front door, relieved to be away from their eyes once he reached the porch.

Old Jim was right. The rain was falling in buckets from the sky and was streaming in waterfalls from a low canopy which was hanging over the front door. It pinged loudly off metal tables and chairs and crashed into fast-moving channels along the edges of the footpaths. Across the road, the smooth stone walls of St. Joseph's Church glistened against the night and cars crawled in slow formations as their wipers flung water from one side to another.

Looking on glumly from beneath the canopy, Cian wondered how indeed he would make it home without being completely saturated. He could order a taxi, but having already broken the twenty euro note, it seemed a luxury too far. He would have to make a dash for it. And so, zipping up his light jacket to the neck, he took a deep breath and rushed out into the street.

Jumping over kerbs and gutters, his runners were flooded instantly, and his toes squelched sorely together. Trying to keep his head up to watch for oncoming traffic, he realised the rainwater had mixed with hair gel and was running down his forehead and burning his eyes. Scrambling for shelter to wipe his face by O'Connell Avenue, he found himself standing beneath the doorway of the red-bricked Sacred Heart Church – all in thirty seconds.

It was no use. The rain was too fierce, and his head was spinning from the run. He was paying double for the whiskey now and a rapid pulse was thundering in his ears. Taking deep gulps of air to slow his breathing, Cian pressed his back against the church door and decided he would wait a few minutes for any sign of a let-up. Gradually, he felt his heart rate fall and he looked up and down the empty footpaths.

"The Crescent," he murmured to himself, what a beautiful street it still was. He had always loved his mother walking this way into town when he was a child. He remembered toddling along behind her in his sandals and gazing up at the brown bricked Georgian buildings arching around Daniel O'Connell's statue in the centre. She would let him throw a copper coin in the fountain if he promised to be good when they were in town. He wished he could remember one wish he had made. And now, with his back against the church door and looking at the same fountain, he wished he was five years old and with his mother again.

Maybe it was a blessing that he and Eva had been forced to call time on their young relationship. He would be ashamed for her to see him as he was in this moment. In staying behind in Limerick, he had spared her the reality of himself. She would never again have to put up with his childlike ventures to the riverside so that he could have time out on his own. She would never have to put up with his drinking and all the darkness that came with it. She would never have to put up with his moods, his upsets and his hypocrisies. He had spared her his bullshit.

Watching the raindrops twinkle in the fountain, he became strangely contented that he hadn't travelled to Australia. Satisfied that Eva was gone and that he was standing on the street. She had earned the right to have the warm sand under her feet just as he and the old city had earned the right to know something of each other's hearts too.

The rain continued to splash into the gurgling water of Daniel O'Connell's fountain and rush down the features of the proud emancipator himself who stood defiantly above the pool. All about the crescent curved street, an orange glow from the lamps illuminated the sculpture, throwing shadows in gothic spires along the sheen of the brown bricked edifices.

O'Connell stood perfectly still. Silently, and with little movement from either, the young man and the statue looked knowingly toward one another.

The Envelope

The carriage rocked a little while pulling out of Colbert Station and the black of early winter hastened behind the amber glow of the city's street lamps. Now slipping into night, the evening's spell of soft rain had eased and spooled itself into fine cotton clouds of white mist, teasing the edge of the open platform and melting against the flanks of the moving train.

Sliding a grey headphone into the hollow of his left ear, Sammy Edwards allowed the side of his face to press against the glass of the 18.20 Limerick to Heuston Station while watching each vacant bench of the platform drift by in lonesome servitude. It was always best to leave one ear unoccupied – especially on lazy Sunday evenings – so as to avoid missing any important announcements from the friendly digital voice of the female train. Indeed, she had just announced that the next stop would be Limerick Junction, and heaven forbid he would miss his change and wake up in an empty train just as Ireland's lonely railways yawned and closed their weary lines for the night.

Having fallen too sleepy for a scroll through his phone, Sammy listened to the weight of the train hum along the smooth steel of the tracks and felt its faint tremors caress his forehead against the surface of the glass. Before his eyes, beads of moisture snaked in reflective trails from one edge of the window to the next, distorting twinkling lights from the residential buildings which were becoming ever sparser as his train left the city and began to rush into the full dark heart of the countryside.

And what a country, thought Sammy, as he reflected upon his annual trip to the capital. Being the line manager during the expansion of the recycling plant, it had become part of his remit to attend a conference at the company's headquarters at the end of each year. Here – like every

December – he would give a PowerPoint presentation on the plant's performance and highlight various aspects of production which could be tweaked to improve output or lower overall operational costs. Finally, he would attend a team building exercise with other managerial staff where the virtues of trust and loyalty would be championed as the cornerstones of their future personal development.

How he loathed it. Bringing his face away from the glass, Sammy softly pressed the rear of his head into the firm cushion of the seat. But a job was a job. Hadn't it guided him through a recession and reared a small family? Many would be glad of it of course, and providing for his wife and daughters had provided him with a dignity not easily afforded to many less fortunate friends.

The female voice announced that his train had arrived on time at Limerick Junction. He would not need to switch trains after all as his current one would be travelling all the way to Dublin. Had Kate not told him he would stay on the same train when she booked the tickets? He either wasn't listening or couldn't remember, and exhaling lightly through a corner in his lips, he wondered which reality would irritate her less.

Accompanying these reflections, the quiet and rural platform of Limerick Junction glowed faintly before the pitch black which gathered behind it. The humble station seemed a flickering candle in a rolling ocean of night and several grey figures stood huddled beneath the dim lighting, impatiently stepping from one foot to another as the carriages slowly ground to a halt.

Watching their icy forms step hurriedly inside, Sammy felt a queer blend of joy and guilt as they opened the doors to other carriages. He had enjoyed the silent company of his fellow solitary travellers and wished for that tranquil atmosphere to continue beyond his journey's first stop. And so, settling back into the warm embrace of his headrest, Sammy listened to the wheels turn once more as the train snaked slowly away from the old station and back to the envelope of the night.

The remainder of his journey might take the bones of an hour and a half, he mused, before grumbling at the sound of the carriage door rattling open behind him – someone had arrived to disturb his peace after all. Heavy footsteps accompanied the squeaking wheels of a well-travelled suitcase along the carpet before pausing behind his ear. The momentary silence was uncomfortable and broken by the startling announcement of his name: "Sam Edwards – by God it's yourself, is it?" boomed a voice of some depth and authority.

Opening his eyes with a jolt, Sammy quickly turned his head toward the sound. Here –towering above him – Frank Molloy smiled warmly through the bristles of his thick black beard. "Long time no see, Sammo – mind if I join you?"

This was indeed a surprise. Sammy had rarely seen his classmate since they left school almost twenty years ago. Managing a weak reciprocal smile, Sammy watched as Molloy shoved his case loudly into the overhead storage rail and unfastened the buttons of his heavy winter coat. While folding the coat neatly beside his case, a sharp aroma of aftershave began to waft notably from under the sleeves of the man's sweater and rained in pungent plumes about the seating area and its small number of occupants below. Once this task was completed to his satisfaction, Molloy tucked in his shirt tails, fixed the seams of his sweater, and brought his considerable bulk to rest behind the table separating himself and his old acquaintance. Finally, he spoke, and when he did – Sammy noticed – he did so with the mild lilt of a Dublin accent: "Jesus Christ, Sammo," "what has it been now – ten years if a day?"

"Oh at least that, Frank."

"And you're looking fresh too, fair play to you. That grey Limerick air mustn't be as poisonous as they make out, what?"

"That's true enough to be sure," Sammy replied quietly, "maybe when you're born there you build something of an immunity to it."

"Not so sure about that now, Sam boy – wasn't I born within an ass's roar of yourself and I couldn't wait to sit my arse on this train many a year ago. One way."

"You're living in Dublin all the time since?"

"Indeed and I am. Malahide for the most part. Was a tough auld station for a few years, but I kept the head down and persevered."

"Good stuff, kid."

Well hard work was never easy as the man says, but after a spell of misfortune I scored myself a cushy number as a field rep for a small hotel chain – if you put in the hours they look after you well, you know?"

He knew. Sammy gazed at the sparkle from the reflective face of his old friend's watch.

"It's just after seven," Frank smiled contentedly, "but tell us anyway – what are you doing with yourself at all these days?"

"I'm still at the recycling plant out on the Ballysimon Road – I'm a line manager now."

Upon hearing this news, Molloy sat forward in his seat and crossed his large forearms on the table top. Keeping his dark eyes fixed upon

Sammy, he knitted the lines of his brow and spoke in a peculiarly hushed tone that seemed befitting of a matter of some importance: "Well I'll tell you something but you're a more patient man than myself – by God, I'd be climbing the walls and frothing at the mouth if I was there for a spell of – ten years now?"

"Coming up on twelve now, Frank."

"Really?" the big man exclaimed. "You know what that is? Loyalty and perseverance to your station – it's not a thing found wanting in Limerick men and I respect that, so I do." Sammy looked quizzically at the assured countenance of his old friend before allowing his gaze to drift to the darkness outside and the reflection of his own tired eyes upon the glass. "I suppose you could call it loyalty. But it's to Kate and the two girls really."

This unexpected development brought about a sudden change in Molloy. "Two girls, you say?" he replied loudly before reaching across the table to clap a heavy hand on the smaller man's shoulder. "Well fair play to you, Sammy old boy – I didn't think you had the stones. And what are their names?"

"Aisling and Siobhán."

"Hah!" Molloy brayed, bringing his palm down forcefully upon the table top. "That's your country now! Two fine Irish names, what?"

"They are I suppose – Kate picked them out before I gave the green light."

"Well, this Kate sounds like a fine woman if you don't mind my saying. And the two girls are healthy, they are?"

"Oh, devil a fear of them."

Opening the cavern of his mouth for another bold statement, Molloy paused mid-breath as the door in the rear of the carriage slid open and a dark-skinned young woman entered behind a refreshments trolley. Keeping his mouth fixed ajar, Molloy raised his large arm and began to twirl his index finger in quick circles. "You'll have a drink?" he asked of Sammy.

"Maybe a coffee if you're getting one for yourself."

The lady arrived at their table and at Molloy's request, promptly placed two disposable cups upon white napkins in front of the men. Handing her a five Euro note for which he requested no change, Molloy grinned suggestively at the young woman. "May the rails rise to meet you, my fair cailín."

Smiling politely, the woman pushed her rattling trolley to the next table while Molloy's eyes trailed her momentarily before returning to his companion with a wink. "A gamey bird if ever I spotted one," he declared beneath his breath. "Now, young Edwards, we'll toast to the prosperity of those two new additions to the Edwards clan, and of course – let it always be said – to the health and wellbeing of your darling mot."

Holding his coffee cup in a mild salute, Sammy nodded his appreciation. "You're a gentleman, Frank."

"Stall the ball now, Sammy boy," Molloy returned with an outstretched palm, "we're not quite ready for a toast of this magnitude just yet, so we're not."

Placing his palms on the table, he lifted his weight slowly out of the seat and into the centre of the aisle where he began to rummage through the front compartment of his suitcase. "Be with you in a tick now, Sam boy," he called from above his companion's head before finally zipping fast his case and awkwardly bringing his large body behind the table once more. Grinning mischievously, Molloy dropped the base of a half bottle of Power's whiskey loudly on the table top. "No harm in making it a bit Irish, what?"

"Ah no, Frank. I've an early start in the morning."

"Era would you give over with that silly talk, man. I haven't seen sight nor hair of you for near ten years and then you come to me with news of a steady and noble mot and a pair of healthy sprogs toddling behind her?"

"I really shouldn't, Frank. I have to find the hotel in Dublin and all yet."

"Sure, we'll be there in half an hour. You'll have an auld drop?"

Pressing the rear of his head against the soft seat, Sammy gazed at the raindrops and felt an oddness in the corner of his mouth as it began to smile reluctantly. "Go on so, I'll have the one – Jesus Frank, you never lost it, kid."

"That's your country," barked Molloy jovially, unscrewing the lid of the glass bottle and generously splashing the whiskey into Sammy's coffee cup. "Give that a good stir now and let it warm the cockles of your heart before we arrive in the auld Pale."

After filling his own cup to the rim, Molloy quickly stirred the liquid with a plastic spoon and raised his toast once more. "To the wife and kids, Samuel."

"Thanks, Frank. And to old friends."

"And to old Limerick," Molloy added with a cackle, "may she ever remain the innocent lady of the Midwest."

Drinking deep, both men brought their cups back to the table and Sammy noticed the sparkle in his friend's eyes as they revelled at the contortion of his face. "Too Irish for you, is that the craic?" Molloy jeered. "You need to get out of stabbers and taste a little of what the good world has on the menu. Be God, once you've drunk black rum on a Jamaican beach you can get back to me, so you can. None of this piss water they sell to dry saps round here, mind – I'm talking real Jamaican black now."

"You've been to the Caribbean?" Sammy inquired, feeling the spark of whiskey flickering to a flame and warming the cave of his belly.

"The Caribbean? I've toured all over the Americas and gave a spell down under too for my sins."

"Was that with the rugby crowd?"

"The rugby crowd? Not at all, young Samuel."

"You went of your own volition so?"

Molloy tilted his chin inward and rested it upon his large neck while considering his companion suspiciously. "Yes, I went of me own volition as you highfalutin Shannonsiders might put it."

"I'd love to see Sydney Harbour myself someday," Sammy mused, looking out the window to the black void.

"Well I'll tell you something for nothing now," Molloy spoke in a hushed tone once more, leaning over the table as if to relay a guarded secret, "they look after you well in this hotel rep gig if you know how to play the game. Sure, I gets penthouse rooms around the globe for business trips a few times a year and not one shilling does it cost me neither."

Sammy felt his jaw slacken as he looked at his friend in some disbelief. "Really?"

"Chalk it down, old son," Molloy grinned, settling back in his seat with an air of satisfaction while watching his companion's eyes stare through the window to the dark. Pausing for a moment, Sammy then listened as his friend's words came at him slowly and deliberately: "There's a lot of deep pockets in that world out there, Sammy boy, you just have to know which ones to reach your hand into."

Over the hum of steel along the tracks, a long silence then broke out between the pair, crackling like the end of a powerful record, leaving its listeners to consider the significance of what they had heard. Discounts around the globe are what Molloy had fallen in for, and Sammy found himself swallowing his sigh deep within his chest so as not to embolden the smirk on his old friend's lips. For all Molloy's bluster, he had nonetheless taken the world for what it had and forged the life he wore with his own hands. He had earned the freedom which he used to traverse the earth, and the attitude that brought him to the top of the tree was the same attitude which allowed him to enjoy its fruits. He would settle for nothing less.

The void had turned to orange as the lights of the capital began streaming past the window and Sammy felt the train slow and shudder beneath his feet. A voice announced their imminent arrival at Dublin Heuston and the shuffle of passengers began in earnest as the carriage sparkled into life from its intercity coma.

"Well, enjoy your short stay with us up here and don't be a stranger," Molloy wheezed as he stretched his arms above his head, "I'm sure the lovely Kate allows you the odd pint when you're away on business?"

"I'll be fairly flat out over the next two days, but we'll see," Sammy replied, forcing his lips to paint a breezy smile.

"Well, you'll find me online and I'll be sure to fix you up with a cheap room for your annual trip next year," Molloy grunted while taking down his case and briskly throwing his coat about his shoulders. "Now, I've got a friend parked in a taxi rank so I'd better dash."

Holding out his large smooth palm, he waited for Sammy's hand to wrap round it before giving it a firm squeeze. "You're a gentleman as always, Mr Edwards," he growled, "the country couldn't stay afloat without the likes of you." Turning sharply on his heel, the large man then hurried his bulk between the seats along the aisle, leaving a bustling wake of heavy breaths and mixed aftershave spices.

Stepping off the train moments later, Sammy gazed along the lengthy dark platform. Figures walked in solitude upon the sheen of icy flags, silent but for the sniffles in their nostrils and the echoes of their shoes. The Dublin beyond them heaved with quiet possibilities – a looming mass of concrete and unrealised experiences. Seductive, it waited patiently in the gloom as a playground for Molloy and his friends. For Sammy, such liberation would never occur again, and he wondered wickedly if it ever had. He was too young when he had gotten married. He was too young and now his phone was dead.

His phone was dead. Realising that his phone was out of battery and that he had forgotten what hotel he was staying in, Sammy began to panic on his next decision. Where was that hotel? Could be anywhere. Could ask someone. No, they couldn't know. Why hadn't he charged his phone? There was a socket on the train.

It was no use. As he looked back towards home, Sammy released a slow sigh and watched the trail of its mist dissipate to nothing in the cool Dublin air. Walking toward the darkness at the end of the platform, he felt alone at the edge of the world. A faint sprinkle of snow had begun to fall upon the railway and as he gazed at the flakes lodging softly along the tracks, he wondered on their vast distance. The cold steel stretched from his eyes through the dark interior of his country and back through the heart of Limerick.

Reaching into a pocket of his jacket for warmth, Sammy felt his fingers touch a folded sheet of paper, and removing it with stiffening fingers, he held it beneath the lamplight for inspection. The paper had a hotel name written in Kate's familiar calligraphic writing. His heart swooned: Carlton Hotel Blanchardstown. It was those three little words.

A Visitor

Father O'Rourke stood in the rear garden of his parochial house and gazed at his vegetables in their carefully cultivated plot. The cabbage leaves shone in a striking emerald hue beneath the midday sun and the freshly turned soil teemed with the possibilities of renewed life.

Though his vocation in his new parish had only begun two months previously, the young clergyman had felt a disconcerting responsibility towards the small garden since his arrival. He was also under no illusions that the paternal care he had begun to bestow upon the plants owed much to the untimely demise of his predecessor – the affable and most reverent Father James Flanagan.

The parish of Galbally had been entrusted to Father Flanagan for over three decades, but at the relatively youthful age of sixty-eight, he had been called to his maker's side once more. It had been sudden. Dr. Joyce had only given Father James the all clear in his annual check-up during the previous month, and by all accounts, he was in great condition for a man approaching his seventieth year.

The post-mortem would conclude that a blood clot drifted to his aorta as he walked out of the post office on the main street of the village. Despite the shock and trauma to those who came upon him as he lay stricken on the pavement, the manner of his death had afforded the man a dignity in its own right – he had died in the embrace of his beloved parishioners – and for that, Father O'Rourke mused above his cabbage leaves, the old priest would surely count his blessings.

The afternoon was turning dark overhead and it had begun to look as if the watering can would prove unnecessary after all. A sharpening breeze bustled through the swaying branches of the apple tree, and as Father O'Rourke looked skyward, he was thankful for the shelter of the high stone walls which surrounded the green enclosure.

Retreating to his kitchen and closing the patio door, the young priest looked solemnly at his phone which lay at the end of a large pine table in the centre of the room. He had left it there deliberately before making good his escape to the garden that morning; yet now that his work had been forced to an abrupt end, he would have to face its incessant demands once more. It was rare that an hour would go by without a notification of some sort or another: a parishioner in need of a service; word of a change to an upcoming event; the bishop to see how he was settling in; or on rare occasions, a message from one of his friends in the city. The message for one o'clock today was from his mother.

It was an unfortunate truth that Mrs. O'Rourke had given three-quarters of her adult life worrying about her children. Her daughter had left home at eighteen to pursue a career in music which remained a work in progress some fifteen years later. She now lived in Birmingham and rarely called home. Mrs. O'Rourke's eldest son had joined the army straight out of school and gave much of his time overseas with the UN on peacekeeping duties. When not in the Middle East he lived near the military base in the Curragh. He rarely came home either unless for a funeral or some other family event he felt compelled to attend. Finally, there was her baby son, her golden boy – and he had run off to join the priesthood.

Father O'Rourke inhaled a tired breath as he picked his phone off the table and read the notification from his mother. There was no pressing news from home, but his personal welfare was still a cause of considerable consternation, and so he began to type his response in earnest. Yes, he was settling in fine and the country people were treating him well enough. Yes, he was eating a hot dinner every day and the housekeeper hadn't made strange with him because of the death of the other priest. And no, he didn't miss the city all that much, but if he did, he also knew he could throw his hat at the whole thing and move home whenever he wanted.

Father O'Rourke looked skyward for some inspiration regarding his mother. He worried that she worried too much about him. It was uncomfortable to think that his father still worked long hours at the factory and that she spent too much time ruminating alone in the house. He would stay an extra hour or two when he drove home for dinner this weekend and embark on a charm offensive on the delights of life in rural Ireland. He knew his mother didn't trust country people. She could never trust people who seemed so closely related or could sleep in their beds without the noise of traffic. It didn't help that her first cousin from Tipperary had something of a roving hand whenever he was around her and could be a little too fond of the drink.

While turning over these considerations, Father O'Rourke became vaguely aware of a door opening at the front of the house and heavy footsteps trampling along wooden floorboards. A trance-like state had rendered him dumb and it was not until the brass handle of the kitchen door turned sharply downward that he became fully aware of his housekeeper entering the room behind him.

Mrs. Fleming bustled into the kitchen with the air of someone who thrived on the virtue of staying busy. With just enough time between breaths to greet the young priest, she quickly moved her large body between the cupboards and the fridge as she stuffed each shelf with food items. The scene brought to Father O'Rourke's mind the motion of a round bumblebee traveling from one plant to another, and he smiled softly to himself at the thought.

"Awful bad turn in the weather, Father Sean," the housekeeper chimed with her head beneath the sink and a rotund rear facing the priest.

"They're giving it bad for the weekend, Mrs. Fleming."

"Well, sure I suppose it had to break sometime, and wasn't God good to give us such a glorious April?"

Father O'Rourke often wondered if his housekeeper made religious references to other people too or if they were exclusively reserved for him. "Sure, God is good to us all, Mrs. Fleming."

"And do you know something else, Father? The sun always shines more in the county than it does in the city – have you ever noticed that?"

"Not really to be honest."

"Gospel truth now, Father. I thought you might have taken heed of it, being a city man and all."

"Well, I suppose the weather has been fairly tropical since I arrived here alright, but it's only been a few weeks."

"Sure, there you go now, Father. You should keep a note of the temperatures and pressures and whatnot in one of those notebooks you do carry on yourself. I'd bet a pretty shilling there's more to what I'm saying than those weather boys on the television do be letting on to."

"I'll make a note of it, Mrs. Fleming."

The housekeeper nodded her approval as she removed a bag of potatoes from under the press and brought them to the sink to be washed. Father O'Rourke didn't like asking what she was making for dinner as it made him feel infantile. While wondering exactly why this was the case, he found his thoughts interrupted by the loud ringing of the doorbell.

"Are you expecting guests, Father?" Mrs. Fleming asked without turning her large back from the sink.

"As a matter of fact, I'm not," replied the priest with a doubtful tone, "you stay as you are – I'll go and see who it must be."

Lifting himself heavily from the chair – for he had become stiff from sitting on the hard-wooden surface – Father O'Rourke walked disjointedly towards the corridor before tidying up his posture as he approached the front porch. Like the house itself, the heavy oak door groaned under the weight of antiquity, giving each visitor a reassuringly regal reception.

"Good afternoon to you," the priest smiled to a young man standing on the stone steps of the parochial house. And the man was quite young indeed: maybe no more than nineteen. He wore an un-ironed shirt in the manner of someone who wasn't accustomed to wearing shirts very often; his tight navy jacket was striking for its abundance of zips, and his blue jeans hung disconcertingly low around his groin.

"Hello Father," the boy mumbled without making eye contact, preferring to stare at a space behind the clergyman's ear.

"And what can I do for you today, young fellow?"

The boy shifted awkwardly on the steps and kept both his hands buried deep in the security of his pockets. "Well, I'd like to talk to you about a baptism if you're free at all?"

Masking his surprise with another smile, Father O'Rourke nodded and once again considered the young man's age. "I'm free right now if you'd like to come in and tell me what arrangements you had in mind?"

The young man seemed at once agreeable to this proposal and looked at the priest directly for the first time. His long fringe was combed carefully to one side and though his pale eyes were tired, his skin was glowing pink and his cheeks flushed with the bloom of youth.

Making their way towards the parlour to the rear of the house, the young man introduced himself as John Brady from Tralee. He had moved from home over a year ago and had been living locally since.

Ushering him to an armchair in the dimly lit room, Father O'Rourke switched on the overhead lights to offset the unseasonably dark turn the day had taken outside the windows. An angry sky boiled in grey clouds over the hills and a heavy air hung in a blanket about the parish.

"A drop of rain would break it," sighed the priest as he brought himself down upon his favourite armchair and opened a large diary for inspection.

The young man didn't answer as his eyes were busily moving through the dark furnishings of the old room. In days gone by, the parlour had entertained many a party, and Mrs. Fleming was quick to discuss which bishops liked a few drops of the hard stuff well into the small hours of the morning. Like the housekeeper's stories, the mahogany cabinets were dated but timeless, and the bottle green wallpaper gave the space a quiet decorum.

"What dates were you thinking of for the Christening, John?" asked the priest.

The young man looked at him dumbly from his distractions. "I'm sorry, what did you say?"

"The baptism, John. What dates did you have in mind for it?"

"Oh, I suppose whatever day suits all of ye up here really."

Father O'Rourke smiled patiently. "I'll need you to be more specific than that. Just give me a rough idea and I'll see what's available here in the diary."

"Oh right. Well, I suppose soon enough, like. Maybe next month?"

"We'd be looking at June so?"

"Yeah, that's grand."

"The 22nd at 1pm suit you well enough?"

John nodded his head in a nervous twitch as if the confirmation of a date had made the occasion a reality he was unprepared for. After giving the names of the mother and child to the priest, he continued to gaze out the window, inhaling deeply into his rising chest and coughing into his sleeve. The rain had finally pierced through the grey blanket overhead and generous drops spattered loudly in the flowerpots on the windowsill.

Father O'Rourke uncorked his fountain pen and scratched the date into the thick paper of his diary. It would be a busy month for him but that was just the way he liked it. So much for twiddling his thumbs by the fireside out in the country. Placing the diary on a low coffee table which sat between them, the priest listened attentively to the rain's melody as it dropped into various containers and chimed against a group of tin cans.

The boy remained unsettled and continued to watch waterdrops snake down the window, his back rigid against the chair. Father O'Rourke became suddenly aware of how little he knew about his guest and parishioner, and this concerned him, for the young man looked tired and troubled in his seat. Feeling a hair bristle against his collar, the priest allowed his voice to fall softly across the room.

"How did you decide upon that name for the baby?"

John looked somewhat startled at his host before painting a smile on his face. "He was always going to be called Dennis."

"Well now, there's a grand traditional name. Dennis, yes – it has a lovely ring to it when you say it aloud."

The young man shifted in his seat and knitted his fingers together on his lap. "It's her father's name and his father before him. She's very close to them both."

"Well, some customs never grow old, and isn't it a blessing that ye have an opportunity to keep the given name in the family?"

John retouched the corners of his painted smile, but his eyes would not twinkle. He sat perfectly still and waited for the next words from the priest.

"And have you settled in well to the village?"

"Sure, I'm doing my best to make a go of it, Father."

"Long way from the kingdom of Kerry up in these parts, I suppose. Still, it's a beautiful part of the country too. And where are ye living if you don't mind my asking?"

"We're sharing a flat on the Tipperary road, but having the one bedroom, it's been a bit cramped the last few weeks with the baby and all."

"Must be a tight squeeze, but sure many a little family has to go through it for a spell."

The young man scratched at the light stubble along the side of his jaw. "Her father has given us a site near their farm about a mile outside the village. The foundations are already dug."

"Oh, sure that's fantastic news altogether, John. Ye won't know yourselves once you have all that room."

"We should be able to move in there within seven months, her father says."

"Well, I wish you both a great future in your new home. Not many young people your age have the opportunity to own their own house."

The young man opened his mouth and hesitated. "I'd best be getting back to herself. I've been gone a few hours and it's getting fairly late in the evening."

Slipping his cap from his pocket, he stood up from the chair and brushed down the front of his crumpled jacket. Father O'Rourke took to his feet as stiffly as before and offered his hand across the table. The young man gazed at the priest's palm momentarily before taking it and holding it tightly. Oddly startled, he looked directly into the priest's eyes. "You'll be sure to come and bless the house now, won't you, Father?"

Before him, the priest saw the image of a child. It had unsettled him since his visitor came through the door, but he could not find the right words of comfort the boy needed in his ears. "I'd be delighted to bless the house and all those in it, John."

The young man smiled his gratitude at the priest and held his hand a little more. "Now Father, I suppose I really must be on my way. Orla will think I got lost in the woods."

Father O'Rourke walked the boy to the front door and bade him a kind farewell. Carefully navigating his path down the stone steps, the youth jammed his hands back into the tight pockets of his jeans and hunched his shoulders against the cold. Within seconds, the sound of his footsteps had faded, and his form melted silently into the mist.

Closing the heavy oak door, Father O'Rourke trudged back to the kitchen and sat wearily at the end of the table. Mrs. Fleming had left the pot on the boil and the windows of the patio doors had steamed to a brilliant white. He had forgotten what was for dinner. He had forgotten what was for breakfast. Placing his smooth cheek in his palm, the priest considered the innocence in the visage of John Brady from Tralee. There was a truth behind the circumstances that led him to the door of this parochial house. The boy was a good soul but something in his eyes had frightened him.

The role of the cleric in this new century was a confounding game and Father O'Rourke knew well the fluidity of its rules. How he longed for the certainty of days gone by. For now, the world outside had fogged from clear skies to a white night which pressed heavily against his skull and the patio glass. Looking from pot to kettle, the young priest considered the weight of his parish in the warm air of the room. Between breaths, his vocation slipped to a singular chamber in his heart and he felt the echo stirring deep within his chest.

A phone vibrated loudly on the table and startled the quiet of empty space. It was a message from his mother. Yes, he would visit next weekend. And yes, he was settling in just fine to the countryside. Little by little, it was revealing itself to him.

Minerva and the Star

It was a question of taste. Mixtapes and unrequited advances to an unscrupulous recording industry – as a whole. A conglomerate of insiders and yes men saying no to each demo she had sent in the shape of her heart. If only they would take the time to fling them back over the wall of silence she had become so accustomed to. She may find a sense of closure. Maybe.

It was a question of maybe. Maybe it was better to be born lucky than rich as her father had always said. Maybe if she knew the right people and moved in their circles, she would be heard above the din of guitar strums on the clicking wheel of fortune. Oh, it clicked, but if only it would stop upon one contact, one solid hearing by the right person and not immediately returned to—what was it called in the writing industry? The slush pile. An endless river of observations and silly dreams trampled underfoot to form the pulp of an insipid red wine: Desperation, 2019.

It was a question of vintage. The sham of creating it for oneself. Never admitting the folly of being influenced exclusively by the twenty-first century. Blonde permed curls and skater girls would never fit in a world of craft beers. If she could grow a beard, she would. It was a question of image and how it stalled in *this* bedroom. The full-length swivel mirror in the room's corner jeered her. Here she was. Reflecting upon her reflection. Again. No photographs were being sent with the tapes. The plaid shirt and tousled hair were just for herself.

It was a question of sport. The Irish translation for fun. All sense of self and ego lost in the strings of music. Wasn't that the true origin of her craft? Or had it become something new? A medium through which to be viewed by others? Distorting prism.

It was a question of perspective. She had seen herself through many angles, inverted planes, dysfunctional parallaxes and each of the four dimensions of time and its space. And time had wanted her to step back from the mirror to her music. Music. Where was the guitar? Yes.

It was a question of rhyme. Without reason, a lyric may aesthetically please though echo hollow through the channels of its creator. Echo. Hollow. Through the channels of its creator. Still, lyrics must aesthetically please.

It was a question of time. Its passage and the grooves it carved through the mind and skin. Her reflection had not been kind to either. A tired brain perceiving its fragile host. Silver bands becoming more frequent. Yes, too frequent to pluck. Spiders within the soul and webs upon the skin. About the mouth. Eyes.

Full of questions. Behind which spun reels of images and a life well lived in a body well lived in. Worn and moulded to fit something new. Bespoke. She giggled the word inside and sank into her seat like drunken feet in old boots. Moulded to what? Music. Maybe. It did sound better now that she had begun plucking the cords. It did.

No more questions. Encore.

Jenny

Young Jack lay motionless in his blankets and watched his breath form wispy clouds of steam in the cool nothingness around his head. Outside, the rain had begun to tinkle its sharp fingers against the window, and the forecast for the whole of the coming week made for uncomfortable viewing. Indeed, his jaded television set had informed him that the unseasonably wet conditions were set to continue from Tuesday to the weekend and so on into infinity.

Even lying on one side beneath his bedclothes, Jack could feel the shiver of an early winter rattle up through the base of his spine, bounce about the cavern of his ribcage and clatter his teeth together until the echo rang forth from his mouth. It was weather for the ducks, as his mother would always say. Of course, she always had some old saying from the dark mists of the 1980s, or an unrelated anecdote with a moral twist to ensure he got whatever point she was trying to make. It amazed him how every story from her youth was not a story at all, but rather a cautionary tale that he should fully digest before he laced up his shoes and walked out the front door. The twentieth-century must have been a terrible time for her.

Yet still, here he was in this first flat since he'd hatched and flew the nest, and he wished he'd heeded some of her unsolicited advice. It would indeed have been a good idea to buy a fan heater if there was no oil in the house. And it would have made sense to buy a thick quilt with a good tog rating if all he had were two thin summer blankets which were as hairless and old as his mother's dog. But he had other ideas for his wages.

Dolans' Warehouse had been hopping on Friday evening. Some of the best emerging international DJs had assembled for a night that his youth would never forgive him for if he dared miss it. Between sets, he'd washed back three pills with a few pints of warm lager in plastic glasses until he became more interested in chewing the plastic than drinking the beer within them.

Mousey Blake and a few old lads from Corbally were shuffling about and sure, it was always a good night when Mousey was around. Never any trouble getting sorted for what you needed, and he was a gentleman about giving you one or two on tick if you were stuck for a few bob. Good old Mousey.

It was a pity the night took such a bad turn. Gazing open-mouthed at the orange strobe lights revolving in opposite directions, Jack's gut twisted and the sense of car sickness that he was still prone to in adulthood returned to haunt the pit of his stomach. Rushing from the floor and into a disabled toilet, he cracked his forehead off the mirror before emptying the contents of his belly into the hand basin. He had stayed there, dry reaching for several minutes with the door half open until an unfriendly security man escorted him to the front door.

"Stay walking now, kid." The voice was broken and dark as the city outside. Exposed to its gloom, Jack found himself cold and alone with the street.

At once, his eyes danced above the rooftops towards the week's terminal rainclouds which had begun to softly coalesce into sodden balls of cotton wool. It seemed to echo the mistimed rhythm of his footsteps along uneven pavements as he began the long struggle home. With spite, the flags continued to revolve beneath his feet while shadows curled and reappeared around gutters and dustbin lids; the roads glistening under a film of surface water and the alleyways gurgling with flowing streams of black liquid.

All about the Dock Road and up O'Curry Street, he stumbled over kerbs and fell on car bonnets as water rushed down the channel of his spine. Cursing the skies and constellations, he slid and sliced his shoulder against the rough bricks of Windmill Street for balance as he rounded the corner towards the sanctuary of his house.

Once outside, after a duel with the lock, he made his way up the stairwell on hands and knees and crawled into the carpet of his bedroom. Home.

But if only his night had ended there. If only he hadn't scrolled through his contact list and found Jenny's number beneath his thumb. If only she had been asleep and didn't answer his call to hear him growling and swearing at her. If only she didn't cry out in horror upon hearing that side of him. If only she never knew that side of him existed.

"If only she thought I was a decent man," Jack spoke aloud to the empty room as he derailed his train of thought from three days ago. Jenny hadn't answered any of his texts since that night and he supposed he'd frightened her off. There was no reason for his anger towards her outside of his inebriation. Though he couldn't remember a word of the phone call, the cruelty of his brain ensured he remembered the tone.

Jenny first became a feature in his life five months previously through the haze of a college party in Castletroy. The glimmer from the blonde braids of her hair and that softness which sat deep within her eyes had drawn him to her through the smoke and music of the living room. It seemed odd to him that he would swallow his shyness deep within his chest and speak to her without being given an introduction. At first, she smiled politely to the space behind his shoulder and refused to meet his eyes. The sensation was not novel to him, but gallantly, he waded through the shallow waters of small talk until she unexpectedly grabbed his fingers and kissed him full on the lips.

Full on the lips. No one had ever done that before – not like that. They found a spot to sit on and effortlessly chatted well into the night about everything their minds could conjure.

He walked her home under the amber street lamps of Milford Grange and lapsed comfortably into the silence of familiarity. The sound of her heels on each footpath echoed up the pebble-dashed walls of the old houses and he wondered on the generations of students who had trod on similar paths, in similar circumstances, while traces of their memories beckoned mischievously behind each driveway and lamppost.

Her own driveway loomed in the quiet of darkness, and when she stopped at its entrance, he could faintly perceive the silhouette of a small palm tree rustling in the cool autumn breeze behind her face. Transfixed as he looked upon each soft feature beneath the half moon, he sensed the caverns of his soul illuminate beneath the lighthouse of her eyes. Locked and magnetised to her visage, he held her gaze until each breath began to quicken and his heart thumped loudly in his ears. They kissed again and it was softer still, inflaming his senses, which were glowing red embers, sparkling and scorching new memories deep within his brain. And then, pulling her lips slowly away from his, she smiled and gently released her grip on his hands.

He watched on helplessly as she walked to the entrance of the front porch while his feet grew new roots on the concrete path. Alas, turning the key in the lock, she stepped inside, blew a warm kiss along the breeze toward him and closed the door. He listened intently as she rotated the lock and flicked a switch, returning the house to darkness.

The walk home was on clouds rather than footpaths and he found his lips making the same shape as the crescent moon. The night was pleasant, and the air of experience hung warmly around his face. He knew that the evening he had shared with Jenny would always be with him and he felt odd about the change it had made inside his skin. As if he had grown from the impulse of boyhood to something approaching a steady state of reason. And he thanked Jenny for that.

He thanked her for many things now as he lay in his bed and gazed blankly at the ceiling. Like always, his words of gratitude formed as notions drifting through his head rather than words upon his lips. If he had thanked her more? Maybe he could send her another message and ask if they could stay friends? It may change down the road. He was pathetic. He was bargaining. It was a stage of grief.

The night in Castletroy began to feel many moons away and the chill of his room sat grim and real in his bones. Rising from the sickly cocoon of his blankets, Jack felt the itch of three days' neglect burning between his inner thighs and his groin. While wallowing in a cool sweat, he had lain in a state of disgrace and decrepitude. Had three days really passed? The air sat heavy with his own organic waste and his lungs begged for the breeze of the river. Yes, he would go to the Shannon.

Remaining unwashed, Jack pulled a hoodie and tracksuit pants over his naked body and found his runners beneath the bed. It was time to go back into the night.

The mist had picked up to a spitting rain and the wind rolled in waves along the Shannon's jagged surface as he made his way down the steps from Sarsfield Bridge to Honan's Quay.

The grey walls of the old bridge loomed large and heavy in his heart while he followed the trail of the river's verge, feeling the chilly hands of autumn on his spine and pulling his hood closely around his face.

As he watched two huddled figures emerge from the park, Jack began to lean against the railing above the water, allowing an acceptance of the dark vista to fall before the curtains of his eyes. The street lamps from Clancy's Strand twinkled across the river in distorted rays, mounting high crests and dancing on white foam as the fullness of the moon pulled the river from the city's heart to the cold indifference of the ocean.

Craning his neck towards the grey mass of King John's Castle, he heeded the girl's advice and allowed his thoughts to fall freely from his lips. They fell in broken utterances of sound and tingled on his tongue as they slid from his face. They dripped from his eyes in salt to the relentless currents of fresh water below where the tides would carry them to Foynes and further out to the infinite Atlantic beyond. A galaxy of tears heaving along the compressed rocks of the seabed and tickling the harbours of New York.

The world swayed on its axis and Jack tightened his grip on the damp metal of the railings. Seasick and lost, he felt the quays' lightbulbs burst and dim within the eye of his mind. Flickering as they receded from the luminance of life and into black once more.

April 1919

Long live our Soviet. Long live the journey of October's revolution into the dawn of a Limerick spring. Long live the resolve of our workers, our merchants, our city, our shared realm – untethered from the occupied island of our ancestry. Long live the aspirations of our brothers and sisters to liberate our motherland from imperial serfdom and shame.

We declare our statehood to be as true as the recent passing of an imperial bullet between the 6th and 7th ribs of our brother Robert Byrne – an honourable postal worker and proud son of Dublin and Limerick. The manner of his death while incarcerated by agents of the crown is indicative of British attitudes towards political prisoners on this island – an island shorn of many young souls on their behalf in the recent European war.

The council stands firmly against the wheel of conscription to aid a foreign military in achieving the ambitions of its empire. We refuse to partake in misadventures on the continent to further the subjugation of native populations around our planet. We purport that all humans are equal citizens of the world.

The Soviet honours the role this city has played in the recent struggles for Irish emancipation. We have stood in solidarity with our brothers during the Dublin lockout of 13 – a righteous attempt by the working classes to receive conditions and payments commensurate with the fruits of their labour. We have fought and lost sons during the Rising of 16 including those executed in Kilmainham Gaol and we honour the memories of our two fallen leaders from that insurrection: Con Colbert and Edward Daly – the youngest revolutionary to face the firing squad.

We reject all attempts to enforce martial law upon our streets and the related suppression of the free movement of citizens. The suffocation of our commerce through enforced isolation shall no longer go unchecked. The soviet's people shall continue to walk freely on the soviet's roads. Our merchants shall trade under our banner and former crown taxes will come under the ownership of the council on behalf of the workers of this city.

Until the establishment of free trade with outside partners is normalised, we shall print an independent currency in denominations of one, five and ten shillings. Each note will be signed in lieu of payment by both the Trades Council Treasurer - Mr James Casey, and its Chairman - Mr John Cronin. A list of reliable traders who accept the soviet's currency will be printed and distributed daily. Any business who engages in profiteering on the back of food or supply shortages will be regarded as an enemy of the Soviet and can expect repercussions consistent with that status.

The Limerick Trades and Labour Council will continue to ensure both the personal welfare and work standards of craftsmen are maintained. We declare that the hand reigns superior to the cog and we will reverse the unnecessary mechanization of our labour in mills and ports. The related disenfranchising of our workers and the dignity of their employment will no longer remain unaddressed.

We propose freedom of religious expression. The Irish experience of centuries of sectarian tyranny makes us unique amongst our red European allies. All religions and none may be practised within our boundaries, though as a people we remain profoundly Catholic.

Since the founding stone was set on the banks of the Shannon and through a subsequent fusion of Norse and Gaelic blood, this city has served as a proud trading post on the outer fringes of a fractured Europe. We have withstood sieges, signed unfaithful treaties, defied the Orange King and stood as the last outpost of Catholic resistance on this island during land seizures and religious suppression. And it is in that honourable tradition that we now declare ourselves the first outpost of Irish egalitarianism in full assurance that the rights of the labouring classes will at last prevail.

God save Ireland. Long live the Soviet.

- LTC 1919

Spanish Point

The envelope had arrived on Friday. It was now Sunday and still it sat on the coffee table in the living room – going nowhere. What was it about the way in which the words were written? Surely the same secretary wasn't still working in the school after all these years? The watermark of *Laurel Hill FCJ* was still the same too, and Amy remembered how she loathed the whiff of pretension from its curling edges. Its tone almost mocked the recipient as the envelope would invariably contain bad news: summer and Christmas reports; absenteeism; notice of impending suspension; money required for sports kits; money required for everything else.

And now – after all this time, that watermark and that envelope had invaded her adult life. It had not passed through her parents' letterbox, but instead made its way across town, into suburbia and over the threshold of her own home. How dare it! It had no right, no jurisdiction here in the sanctuary of her own fully mortgaged dwelling. It should be removed at once, flung to the bins and interned in the nearest landfill. It should be cremated in pagan ritual. It should be gone. It should be. It should. But she had opened it and now it was too late. This time, without her parents to punish her, the news within the envelope had warmed her cheeks with a new despair. A new twist at the end of the same old road.

Amy O'Neill pressed her forehead against the wooden panels of the cupboard over the sink. She had forgotten what she had come into the kitchen for and found herself hoping that it wasn't simply to get away from the letter. Surely, she needed a cup of tea? A Club Milk? No, the contents of the letter would have to be accepted. And so, walking downtrodden back to the living room, she fell heavily into the couch behind the coffee table and gazed at the envelope's torn edges once more.

The daylight had yielded to dusk outside her window and the lights of Dooradoyle twinkled against the dusty red glow of the city beyond. "Shepard's delight," she whispered into the sleeve of her woollen sweater, curling her feet beneath her body to offset the fall in temperature. The timber flooring seemed all the world a desert in the last blaze of the failing sun and its sombre rays illuminated the cherry schemed furniture in a glow of saffron hues.

Beneath the floating dust particles, the envelope waited to be examined once more and it did so with air of finality. Pursing her lips, Amy reached across the table and picked the paper up by the edges. When she first opened it this morning, she had unfolded the letter within and read the first two lines before carefully placing the letter back inside to never be unfolded again. Now, it demanded to have its story told in full before it would leave her in peace. And so, removing the letter once more from its paper case, Amy opened it out again and cast her eyes upon its contents:

Dear Ms. Amy O'Neill,
You are cordially invited to the annual Laurel Hill school reunion, which this year marks the 20th anniversary since the graduation of the class of 99'. We hope you will be in a position to attend and we look forward to seeing you on the night. Please RSVP the school secretary at…

Amy slid back into the warm folds of the couch. Sherry Crowley would be there of course. She'd married that building contractor who had his name in lights on every crane in Limerick. She met him in Australia when she went travelling after college. Dark haired fella. Good hurler in his day – should have made county. And then there was Linda White. Wasn't she in Galway with her husband? He was from the Gaeltacht and his father gave them a site there around ten years ago. She was always good at Irish and the husband was a teacher. Great holidays. And he was a good hurler.

"Ah fuck this," Amy winced, throwing the envelope back to the coffee table. She knew where these ruminations were heading: in circular loops from this moment, in this house, all the way back to 1999. And what of it? Hadn't she a house to ruminate in? And a career at the revenue office? And a nice back garden with decking?

It was an easier life. It was rewarding too in its own ways and she had become set in her own ways. Sure, who would put up with her at this stage anyway? In another's company she could never enjoy her summer evenings practicing set dancing in the living room again; or her winters nights watching pop videos by the fireside – half-naked, sipping hot port and enjoying various soft cheeses.

Yes, yes, it was better this way. Better to be the skipper of one's own ship and the navigator of choppy seas. And how the crests and troughs had rolled her round the island's coast, but never too far. She had never left Ireland – at least not in a meaningful way. She always steered close to the shore and kept the comely green hills in eyeshot. The blue horizon was exhilarating to ponder but frightening to navigate without a chart.

She remembered first pondering these things as a girl when she sat on a warm rock by the ocean in Spanish Point. The sea stretched a million miles beneath the sun's bright glare, and each ripple from the coast to the edge of the sky glistened like silver trinkets tumbling through the water. A sprinkle of sail boats dotted the wide horizon, their brightly coloured masts sitting meekly against the vast blue surface of the ocean. "What wonder," she spoke aloud in the wonderment of a child. "What comes after that blue line and how far away is New York?"

"Too far to swim," replied her father, who sat himself stiffly down upon the rock beside her. He had brought them to Spanish Point every summer for a few days. And just as sure as carrots were important for her eyesight, an annual exposure to the Atlantic air was vital to keep a girl's hair curly, or so she was always told.

"But you could swim it, Daddy, couldn't you? If you really had to?"

Her father chuckled, rubbed the furrows of his bristled cheek and placed a firm arm around his daughter's back. "Sure, I'd do my best the same as anyone else, Amy."

She knew he would. He always would.

"But you know," her father continued in a wistful voice that usually signalled the beginning of a story, "I might not have to make it the whole way to America at all. There's something we don't always see sitting out there where the sky meets the water and does a dance with the fairies."

Amy looked to where her father was pointing but could see nothing beyond the blue water and air. "Could I see it if I got a boat to take me there?" she asked.

"You might, but a white horse would be even better."
"You mean a sea horse?"
"Well, yes, I suppose I do. But a big one that would carry you."
"And where would the sea horse bring me, Daddy?"
"To that island of the fairies: *Tír na nÓg*."

Upon hearing the name of this strange island, Amy sat back in her father's arms and listened to the story about the land of the fairies: the land of youth where no one ever grew old. He told her of the warrior Oisín, who fell in love with a fairy named Niamh, and of how she had convinced him to leave his family in Ireland and travel on a white horse across the sea to Tír na nÓg. And there he stayed for 300 years.

All the while, as her father spoke, Amy trained her eyes on the edge of the horizon. Maybe if she tried really, really hard, she would be able to see it.

The trip to Spanish Point was always the highlight of the summer. They would stay in a rented mobile home park at the edge of town. By day, Amy and her younger sister would play with the other children on the beach, picking seashells and building castles with moats for the eternal storylines of the prince and princess. At night, they would watch movies and play card games way past 'Limerick' bedtime, until her eyes drooped, and she fell asleep in her chair. There would then follow the light sensation of being hoisted up in her father's strong arms and being swept off to the bed with a final tickly kiss on her cheek from his bristles.

It was different in Limerick. He would always come home from work after her mother had finished the bedtime story. She knew they hadn't a lot of money and that this had something to do with her father being away for so long. She would hear them talking downstairs in the kitchen sometimes and she wished she could get up and see him before she fell asleep. But that would get her in trouble of course and no one had time for that.

But her father always had time in Spanish Point. Time for her mother and sister. Time to enjoy the sea air, go fishing or take long walks by the cliffs. Time to find himself in the company of his family, as if time itself meant nothing at all.

"But Oisín became bored after 300 years," her father continued. "He loved Niamh, but he longed to return to Ireland and see his people once more.

Amy began to narrow her eyes towards the horizon, she could almost swear she could see Oisín on his white horse in the haze of the white clouds which skirted the edge of the sea. She then listened as her father told her of the greatness of Oisín's sorrow upon his return, as he realised all the centuries that had passed. For it meant that his family were gone, long dead, and Ireland itself had forgotten their names. How Oisín cried for his father and mother and for his hounds. How he thought of his father's last words to him: that they would never see each other again

– a father now bones in a grave. For time had meant something: it had meant a thousand farewells never spoken. And when Oisín fell from his horse, he too, would feel the wasting of time upon his ancient body and would die in the arms of a stranger.

Clinging to her father's arm, the girl felt the weight of her years come suddenly upon her: the weight of her memories complied over so many seasons; the weight of Ireland, which had always drawn her to its soil, and within a fever, she awoke as an adult on her couch in Dooradoyle.

The room was still, and her father had gone. He had been gone a long time. Amy felt a bubble of water erupt from beneath her right eye and a single hot tear scorch down her cheek to the top of her lip. The saltwater between Spanish Point and the fairy land tasted bitter on her tongue and she shut her eyes tightly against the sickness of it all.

Her house reposed in an earthly silence and the air hung heavy with the weight of another summer. Twisting beneath a blanket of humidity, her ears listened for the faint sounds of the living which might emanate from outside her singularly occupied space. Behind the door, a timid breeze rustled in the letterbox and a grandmother clock ticked its life away to a lonely hallway. The kitchen sat in a cold and clinical stillness, broken only by the sound of an insect hitting the patio glass and the internal humming of the fridge. All around, the solitude of the quiet set deep within her home as the walls slowly creaked and the house began to settle.

She would return to Spanish Point. Not tomorrow, but now. Rising from the couch, Amy stepped heavily on each foot until she found herself in the kitchen. Sliding her keys from the countertop, she stepped loudly along the wooden floorboards of the hallway to the front door. But now, closing her hand tightly around the bunch of keys, she hesitated at the lock.

Looking back to the living room, Amy could see the letter from her school still sitting on the table. The invitation to commemorate the decades of her life and a drawing nearer to the earth of old Ireland. Turning from its words, she flung the door open and felt the cool summer's breeze flow over the contours of her face.

She would return to the white horse of Spanish Point. And her feet would never touch the soil again.

A Study in F

The air was fresh and the high buildings of Henry Street were unusually quiet for half-past eight on a Tuesday morning. It had occurred to Peter Carson, that the particular block where the plush Savoy Hotel faced the white modernity of a multi-storey carpark was beginning to resemble something of architectural note. Each building consisted of roughly six or seven floors which obscured the blue of the morning light, giving a paired down Manhattan feel to the eye of only those who dreamed such things. Then again, the famed grid system of New York's streets had been modelled on that of Limerick, and Peter felt very intelligent for knowing this. Indeed, there were many obscure facts about the city which he had collected from his forty-five years of living within it and he would often use these to regal the few people in his life with whom he felt comfortably acquainted.

Approaching the corner of Roche's Street, a southern wind whipped around the corner of a stone building and Peter instinctively wrapped his overcoat around the dimensions of his slight frame—wondering aloud if he should have worn a hat. He had always been somewhat fearful of wearing hats, for he had heard that they may bring about the onset of premature baldness. His wispy brown hair, though somewhat faded, had, for the most part, remained attached to the top of his head; though on breezy mornings such as this, he wondered if the sudden gusts may nonetheless cause irreparable damage to his brittle follicles for no other reason than to spite him.

Arriving on time to the front door of Harper's solicitors' office, Peter paused to look at his reflection in the glass panel. His pale complexion pained him somewhat, yet he could never consider sunbeds; what with their coffin-like nature being aptly infused in their carcinogenic radiation. Yet he knew he needed to breathe colour upon his skin in some form. His white cheeks had sunken somewhat and his jawline had begun to droop a little along its former sharp edges. Considering the contours mournfully, he watched his sad eyes examine the face they were set in, but they too had lost something of their lustre and moved dully in the ageing visage faintly reflected upon the glass.

Oh, my word, he thought, entering the reception area of the office and typing a code which would bring him around to the other side of the desk. It was better not to get too caught up in such pointless musings. After all, little could be done to slow the process and were he to do something radical such as surgery, people would notice. Had he not seen enough cases involving knives in his work at a solicitors' office in Limerick to last a lifetime? Peter smiled to himself when he thought of this. He was very clever.

The clerk's desk was behind a large glass window in the reception area of the dated office, and it was from here he took care of all administrate duties for Harper's Solicitors and Associates. Beyond his glass window sat a quaint and narrow waiting room of fading 1970s' décor: its dark timber furnishings only offset by the occasional cream cushion or sprig of green from a potted plant. A silver CD player sat awkwardly in its timber surroundings and wafted the tones of RTE's morning radio up through the crackling Venetian blinds which swayed to a summer dance with an unseen open window.

The scene was a deliberate construct of Peter's notions on blissful environments and helped immensely in the administration of his secretarial workload. Though this work was exclusively clerical, it was not without an aura of prestige, and Peter often postulated that unlike the solicitors, he was the one crucial cog which never needed oil. For by their nature, attorneys were required to exist in a vacuum of massaged egotistical facades—whereas Peter was a creature of more simple requirements.

As if to confirm this conjecture, Peter heard the familiar clack of one of his boss's high-heeled shoes echo from the pavement outside the front window and within seconds Brenda Harper had bustled into the reception area, both hands full with briefcases and various paper folders. Hurried and confused, her eyes quickly focused on her assistant who was sitting with an air of some contentment behind his glass panel.

"Get me the McGinley files at once please," she whistled through gasping breaths, which laboured from the efforts of an unhealthy fifty-year-old body. Peter winced a little at the sharpness of her tone. Though he was rarely intimidated by Brenda, his subordinate role became more pronounced in the midst of a crisis. He also disliked the glare that she threw in his direction which suggested that he was in some way responsible for her poor timekeeping. Her hazel eyes, which were still beautiful, sat coldly in the round dimensions of her face; and like the dry brown hair which hung past her shoulder, didn't flit a moment until Peter began to look a little more spritely.

"Oh, bloody hell, he's here already," hissed Brenda beneath her breath as the sound of the outer door's movements echoed into the reception room. With little time to consider much else, the solicitor piled her cases and files on a slim chair and turned to face her favoured client who had officially arrived two minutes early.

"Good morning, Mr. McGinley," she smiled through her dark red lipstick.

James McGinley entered the room in a brisk and business-like fashion, stretching his hand to offer the customary firm handshake. "And a rather pleasant morning it is too, Brenda," he grinned, flashing the white veneer of his front teeth. Mr. McGinley was an imposing bulk of suit and flesh, whose presence filled a room as quickly as his duty-free aftershave. His thick neck overflowed in the shape of a solid ring above a well-tailored shirt collar, and the sheen from his slicked-back hair gave the disconcerting aura of a halo.

Towering over Ms. Harper as they shook hands, McGinley rolled his eyes sideways to address her employee. "Carson, isn't it?"

"Yes, Peter Carson."

"Well Carson, is there any truth in this rumour I hear knocking about?"

"What rumour are you referring to, Sir?"

"What rumour? Why that story I've heard about you going to make me a strong cup of tea?"

Peter looked at the man somewhat dumbly.

"Well?" McGinley raised his voice and looked to Ms. Harper whose smile remained firmly embossed upon her pale cheeks.

Peter continued to gaze perplexed at the man. "So," he hesitated, "you wish for me to make you a cup of tea?"

Placing his hands upon his large hips, McGinley theatrically gaped about the room for support from an imaginary audience. "Why yes, Peter, if you would be so kind?"

Turning about in his small office space to find the key for the kitchen, the clerk was finally rescued by Ms. Harper, who assured McGinley that Peter would bring the tea through to her meeting room as soon as he had it brewed.

The situation seemingly resolved, Ms. Harper thanked Peter and walked into her office, leaving the door open for McGinley to follow. However, waiting for her to leave earshot, McGinley placed his well-shaven jowls half an inch from the glass which separated the waiting room from the reception desk. "Still though," he whispered, "I don't blame you for being a little slow on the uptake, old chap. The life of a manservant must have a terribly dulling effect on the senses."

Suddenly ceasing his search for the kitchen's keys, Peter stood in the centre of his reception office and spoke with uncertainty: "I don't really understand what it is you are referring to, Mr. McGinley?"

"Ah Peter, we're all friends here—what is it, twenty odd years you've been sat behind that desk serving Brenda? Terribly unnatural state if you ask me, though I guess a person will do what they must to earn a living. Tell me this though—just between us boys—you must have had awful potent fantasies about the old girl from time to time? All that power she wields over you on a daily basis? She's still a bit of a looker too in the right light."

Mr. McGinley, I really don't think that is…" Peter began.

"I'd have myself rubbed raw so I would, and there's no shame in it," continued McGinley, "go on, Carson, tell me—it must be fierce intense alone after a bottle of wine of a Friday night?"

Without taking his eyes from the folded stack of papers which lay on his desk, Peter spoke lowly, in shame at the tone of McGinley's conversation: "I am perfectly sure that I have no idea what it is you are referring to and I do wish you would refrain from speaking to me in such a manner, Mr. McGinley."

"Era, have it your own way, man. All I'm saying is that it's a funny way to spend a career. Still and all, your name is Carson I suppose—maybe it's the Protestant work ethic coming out in you what?"

With that, McGinley winked mischievously and brought his bulk away from the counter, "Go easy on me, Peter, sure I'm only having the sport with you," he smiled before stepping heavily into Ms. Harper's office and closing the door behind himself.

Peter gazed a moment at the dark wooden door of Brenda's office which seemed peculiarly ominous in the sudden silence of the room. A black metal plaque with silver trim had been riveted to the timber which proudly declared the credentials attained by Mses. C. and B. Harper during the formative years of their legal careers in University College Cork. It came to Peter's mind that he had never fully understood the meaning behind the various acronyms which proudly validated the sign's authority.

Continuing to busy his hands by moving paperwork, he tried not to ruminate over McGinley's words which were ringing loudly in his ears. Yes, he had referred to him as a manservant rather than a clerical worker. Maybe he was two steps away from being a lady's lackey and one gender change from a secretary. No, he was letting McGinley get to him.

An hour passed under such considerations and little work was completed despite its mounting necessity. Beyond the glass, the radio in the waiting area told the same news on the half hour and took calls from a discontented public to fill the gaps between. Above the silver CD player, the Venetian blinds continued to flit in front of an open window and the large potted plant danced along to the breeze. Feeling somewhat lulled by the monotone tranquillity, Peter gazed sleepily through the gaps of the blind to the concrete and blue skies of the city outside. Here, the people walked the streets with purpose; their errands setting the foundations of greater plans which even if never fully realised, created meaning in the lives of their hosts. In every mind, a scaffold to a greater existence was being held in place with old rope. And they would each climb it too—level by level until finally, the lights went out.

"Are you alright Peter?" Ms. Harper stood in front of the glass with her black folder held tightly to her chest. Dazed, Peter realised he had been drifting half to sleep and not noticed the door to her office opening.

"Yes, Brenda, sorry I was just thinking about something."

"Well snap out of it please," she whispered, "Mr. McGinley is walking out behind me."

As soon as she had spoken, McGinley appeared at the door. "You never brought me my tea after all that hullabaloo?"

That was right. In all his distractions he had forgotten about the tea. "Sorry about that, Mr. McGinley, I received a phone call after you went in and forgot about it," Peter replied sheepishly.

McGinley made his way to the counter and pressed his face near the glass as before. "It's quite alright, old chap," he grinned in a mocking upper-class accent, "must be awfully hard to find good help these days, what?"

Peter looked at McGinley's sneering round visage in disgust. His shirt collar had already darkened around the rim with sweat from the roll of his overhanging neck and his milky eyes looked sinister and dirty in their sockets. His overbearing aftershave had infused with the gas of fried eggs from his breath and the hybrid stench reeked through the holes of the glass and into Peter's workspace.

"Well, Mr. McGinley," Peter began, his cheeks ablaze in the fires of indignity, "if you are in such need of regular hot refreshments then might I suggest that you bring a flask in your briefcase for future engagements?"

"What was that, Carson?" McGinley growled menacingly.

Trembling, Peter looked viciously at the man and felt a surge of blood begin to boil over in his veins. "Oh, go and make your own bloody tea!" he exploded, jumping to his feet and knocking over a stack of carefully organised folders. McGinley wheeled backwards in a defensive reflex at the sudden outburst.

"Peter!" Ms. Harper exclaimed and immediately began consoling and apologising to McGinley who stood somewhat dumbfounded in the centre of the room.

"Never in all my years," he began muttering under his breath while staring perplexed at the thin rod of rage that was now Peter Carson behind the glass.

"I don't know what in heaven's name has gotten into you, Peter; but you would do very well for yourself if you offered an immediate apology to Mr. McGinley—do you hear me?"

Peter looked from the stern face of Ms. Harper to the open-mouthed gape of McGinley and felt the temperature cool around the surface of his forehead. It had been years since he'd lost his temper and he had forgotten how blindingly debilitating it could be. White stars still fell around the room before his eyes and his brain had turned to a thick stew incapable of reasonable function.

"I'm sorry," he blurted automatically.

Ms. Harper, still clutching McGinley's jacket sleeve glared scornfully at her assistant. "Take an early lunch, Peter."

"But I need to tidy up this mess back here," Peter spoke while looking at the table.

"Just go."

Realising there was little to be gained by arguing, Peter came out from behind the glass and walked past both silent figures to remove his coat from the rack which stood in the corner of the room. McGinley continued to look on with a slacked jaw as the clerk passed by him. He had done this since the outburst and continued to do so as Peter left the reception area, closed the glass door, and walked out into the yellow sunlight of the street.

Jaywalking across three lanes of Henry Street's crawling vehicles, Peter loudly cursed the sun upon his neck while inhaling tarmac and exhaust fumes through his open mouth in the process. Removing his coat at the far side of the road, he trudged gloomily up the cream flags of the pedestrianised Bedford Row, before turning once more into the loud traffic of O'Connell Street.

It was time for a drink. Peter seldom drank on weekdays and only moderately with his friends at the weekend. The meticulous order of his life would not allow for the disarray of intoxication nor the lethargy of a hangover. His time was a precious currency to him, and he wished to spend it with his facilities operating at an efficient level. Nonetheless, there was today. Yes, he assured himself, a liquid lunch would wash the morning down the urinal of his memory.

Crossing the top of O'Connell Street, he made his way into the cool porch of the White House Bar and pushed in the glass panelled door. The space inside provided an instant sanctuary from the bustle of the street. He noted how light made its way softly through the frosted glass and fell dimly around the dark timber furnishings which were spread evenly throughout the room. Empty booths sat waiting for patrons on either side of the walls and the tall bar was complimented by high stools with thick backrests and green leather cushions. The lure of the public house, thought Peter, as he approached the bar and considered a pint of ale and the curse of Ireland.

The barman was a young chap of college going years who sported a well-trimmed beard and a haircut which remained unfathomable to the middle-aged. His thick-rimmed glasses sat casually on the bridge of his nose, and peering over the top of them, he addressed Peter while pushing a noisy tray into a washer. "Can I get you something, Sir?" "A pint of stout, please—Beamish."

"No problem, take a seat and I'll drop it down to you when it's ready."

Peter thanked the surprisingly polite young man and made his way over to an empty table which directly faced the counter. He had decided to forego his usual ale for a stout as he surmised that, as it was lunchtime, it would be better to have something that had eating and drinking in it. Beamish was also a little cheaper.

When the young barman placed the settled pint of stout in front of him, Peter visibly licked his lips in thirst. Teasing himself by looking at the beads of condensation snaking down its black sides, he put his hand on the cool glass and brought it to his face. The scent of malt and hops tickled the tip of his nose a little before he drove it deep into the stout's creamy head and drank deeply.

The thirst broke, he brought the glass down on the table top with a reassuring clang and exhaled in reckless abandonment. He was very naughty. Twelve o'clock in the day of a Tuesday and here he was drinking a pint of stout. But why was he here and how had he gotten himself into so much trouble? Brenda was livid and now he genuinely had to fear for his job. He shouldn't have let McGinley get under his skin that way. In any event, his reaction was completely disproportionate and out of character. Was there even some truth in McGinley's oafish words? Maybe he really was little more than a manservant—a glorified teaboy for his bosses' whims. More worryingly, as McGinley had suggested, it may be true that he had harboured an odd subordinate fetish regarding Brenda over the years.

Peter took another deep draught of his Beamish and thought about this detail. Really? He supposed she did look somewhat attractive in her business suits and figure-hugging formal dresses. Her deep brown eyes were always something which he had admired, and they had not lost a drop of depth in their vast oceans during the twenty-five odd years he had known her. There were times too—if he were honest with himself—that he had looked down her blouse as she leaned over to give him orders of some kind and he couldn't swear that he had not become aroused in the moment. Of course, that was the point, wasn't it? She had been giving him orders at the time.

Peter drank another large gulp of stout and began to feel embarrassed for himself. It was true that on some level he certainly drew pleasure from Brenda's superiority over him. Did this make him dirty? What sort of man had he become? McGinley had done much to emasculate him in a short time this morning and he cursed the brute and all who entertained his withering bile. Draining the last dregs from his glass, Peter approached the counter for another swift one.

"Same again?" asked the young barman.

Peter ordered another Beamish and accompanied it this time with a whiskey chaser. The barman duly obliged and when the Beamish had settled, he placed both glasses beside one another on the dark wooden countertop. Before paying his money, Peter took in a large swallow of stout and quickly followed it with the whiskey till the little glass dribbled its last scorching river onto his tongue.

"That'll put hairs on your chest alright," chirped a voice at the corner of the bar. Peter turned to see a man sitting on a high stool with his elbow on a newspaper. He was about the same age as himself, but he was bulky, and his face was flushed. He had—in Peter's learned opinion—the distinct whiff of an ex-rugby player.

"You up for one yourself?" asked Peter in a congenial tone, though clearly challenging the man.

"Bit early for me, auld pal," replied the other patron, smiling into his lager, "sure wouldn't I be in the bottom floor of the dog house if the wife got the smell of whiskey off me of an afternoon?" Peter considered this reasoning with no small level of scorn.

"Jim O'Grady," said the man, holding out his hand. Peter looked at the sweaty palm and large sausage fingers for a moment before shaking it reluctantly.

"Peter Carson."

"Well, Mr. Carson, it's not a bad auld day, what?"

The clerk sighed and agreed, sitting down on a stool next to the big man. This is what days in the town were like he supposed. He felt sure that soon they would be discussing sport or whatever scant knowledge O'Grady had picked up about politics and the general state of the country. How many days of one's life could elapse in the intoxicating haze of Limerick's various public houses? Considering his morning, would it be a bad life at all?

O'Grady surprised Peter by sticking to the topic of weather and it turned out that he knew quite a bit about climate change and was conscientious of his carbon footprint. In turn, Peter explained some of the technicalities of the Irish judiciary and the importance of its separation from the elected government of the day. However, as O'Grady was beginning to fully grasp the concept, Peter became distracted by another customer who was sitting in the corner of a booth. This young man wore a baseball hat which was casually placed at a jaunty angle on the side of his head. In his arms, was an acoustic guitar which he had begun to tune with rapid hand movements and the leaning of his left ear to its strings. Excusing himself momentarily from O'Grady, Peter approached the man and asked if he was going to play music in the bar today—an odd thing for a random Tuesday afternoon.

"Unlikely," replied the young man, "I'm only a scrub."

"A what?" Peter asked.

"I'm only busking down the road for the evening like."

"I see." Peter knew how to play exactly three songs on the guitar. He had taught himself in college for the same reasons he now felt growing inside his chest in bubbles of hot air. He wished to impress others along with himself.

"Would you be so kind as to let me try it out?" he asked of the young man.

The busker looked at him somewhat perplexed before answering: "Knock yourself out, kid, but if the barman pipes up it's your own look out, yeah?"

"Of course." Peter returned to his high stool and smiled at the round face of O'Grady.

"You're gonna give us an auld bar?" asked the big man.

"Only one or two," smiled the clerk before adding with a wink, "I've a good job to be getting back to."

Fumbling over the cords, Peter finally found his rhythm and began to pluck away to a Phil Collins number. It wasn't so difficult when one knew how, he thought, as he began to lowly sing the opening verse. His voice, though trembling, held its pitch.

O'Grady grinned drunkenly and raised his arms in a large 'V' above his head before crooning along to the chorus: "It's just another day in paradise."

And it was. Peter played through his full repertoire of three songs, greatly regaling the barman and the other three patrons of the bar.

"There's the man," roared O'Grady, slapping his wide palm on the countertop, "Do ya see you? You're some hero, you, boy!"

Peter felt the warmth of this appreciation begin to flush along the surface of his cheeks. He had taken quite a risk in playing the guitar for he could easily have forgotten the cords and looked foolish. If he only knew more tunes, he would gladly play them; indeed, he would stay for another round or two if work wasn't beckoning his mind to return.

Looking at his watch, Peter saw that it was now almost half past two. He felt Brenda would understand his lateness and put it down to a desire for a well-needed timeout after the morning's drama—however, she wouldn't tolerate a smell of whiskey or the glint of a glassy eye.

Resigning himself to leave his congenial company, the tipsy clerk bade farewell to O'Grady, who tightly squeezed his hand and made him promise he would return next week as Tuesdays were his preferred time for day drinking. The young busker and the barman also shook his hand and smiled roundly at the pleasure it had been to make his acquaintance. Agreeing with all of this, Peter elegantly draped his coat over his forearm and made his way back through the dark wooden doors and out to the dazzling street.

The sun had not given an inch and the disorientating reflections were cruel on eyes which had become accustomed to the cool dimness of an alehouse. At once, Peter decided it would be best to walk around the block by the river—it was longer and the fresh breeze from the water may blow some of the cobwebs from his contented boozy mind. He would also pass a shop in which he could buy a packet of mints. Yes, that would be an important detail.

Coming onto the quays, he watched the swans drift silently along the wide river as a group of seagulls stood on the promenade's railings and eyed each passing human for food. Passing slowly along the timber decking, Peter began to reminisce on the afternoon's merriment. He had impressed O'Grady. Though the probable ex-rugby player was a large man, the unassuming clerk had given him an exhibition in drinking. He felt the two younger bucks—the barman and the busker—had also revelled in his musical entertainment. Again, this was amplified by his outward appearance as a nobody—and nobody had expected it out of him.

With his chin in the air, Peter inhaled the river breeze and placed his hands casually in his trouser pockets. He was a man. If only McGinley could have seen him drink and regale the regulars of The White House, he'd never have cause to question him again. Of course, McGinley was probably a lightweight at the back of all his bluster in any case.

While distilling these considerations, Peter's flow was interrupted by the sudden call of a woman's voice behind him. Turning on his heel and dragged from his musings to reality, he was met with the alarming spectacle of a young woman with her hands in the air and a man running towards him with the trailing straps of a handbag floating from behind his body.

What to do? It felt strange to Peter that his legs seemed to fill with ice at that moment; strange too, that his feet were so cold they froze to the surface of the timber decking. Attempting to free himself, he watched as the woman continued to howl from a distance while the thief came closer to him along the railings of the river. As he approached, the young man slowed and pulled up his hanging tracksuit bottoms, puffing heavily and wiping his sleeve against his nose as he caught his breath. At ten feet, the youth's eyes stared directly at the clerk's, questioning without words and drawing comfort from the response. Cautiously, he crossed the road in front of Peter, turned his face and slipped silently up the darkness of a side ally.

The woman continued to stand motionless on the decking. Around her, a group of seagulls circled and called for help to fill their bellies. Peter stared dumbly at her and wondered if he should say something. Across the road, two middle-aged women with cloth shopping bags moved their heads like tennis spectators between the woman and the clerk. Finally, they made their way to the other side of the road to offer assistance to the young woman who remained rooted to her spot on the path. Nothing more could be done. Turning back in his original direction, Peter made his way around the corner towards the office.

It had all happened very fast, he thought, if he were ready, he would have reacted in another way. He'd had a few drinks and that had dulled his senses. He wasn't used to being tipsy in the daylight and the afternoon had been so bright and dazzling. Any other day would have been different.

Returning to the office, Peter pushed open the door sheepishly and stepped into the cool air being generated by the fan. Brenda stood in the waiting area briefing a client. Noting his appearance with a flick of her eyes, she continued to speak as her assistant opened the side door to his office and took his position behind the glass of the reception area.

Keeping his head down and busying himself, Peter groaned internally as he heard the door open and the client politely leave. At best, he was in for an earful. Listening to the door closing, he sighed at Brenda's steps along the carpet and could smell the faint aroma of her perfume before she spoke: "Where in God's name were you?"

"Sorry, Brenda, just needed a bit of space after this morning," Peter replied gently, glancing up from his papers.

The solicitor looked at him sternly. "You were gone a full three hours and you know well I needed you to proofread those McCarthy letters."

"Sorry again, Brenda, I'll get to it right away."

"That was some display you put on here this morning and..." Ms. Harper stopped mid-sentence and looked puzzled. Bringing her face closer to Peter, she began sniffing the air like a curious animal through the holes in the glass. "Is that alcohol I smell?"

Peter felt his face flush with new warmth. "Well," he stuttered, "I only had the one with my lunch if you don't mind."

Ms. Harper stood back from the glass, her round features twisted in disgust. "I bloody well do mind! And don't you give me that one with your lunch nonsense—it's been three hours and your eyes are dancing in your head."

"Brenda."

"Get a coffee out of the machine in the lobby and sit there until you sober up. I want those files proofread before you leave here today, and I don't care if it takes you till midnight."

"Brenda."

"And God help you and the dot that's missing over an 'i' if I come across it," the solicitor growled before retiring to her office with a final glare, leaving her castigated assistant to stew upon her words.

The sudden silence of the room was quite deafening, and the flushed clerk sank wearily back in his chair. It had been a long day and a longer evening was yet to come. Allowing his ageing body to slump and fill the leather cracks in the seat, Peter listened to the rambling monotone of Radio 1 hissing from a cheap CD player in the corner of his office. Through the glass and into the waiting area, he gazed at the potted plant which sat sadly in its prison on the window ledge. Behind it, the flitting Venetian blinds teased of an unseen window which opened outward to a blue sky full of promise. A world of men. For out there, fallen men sat in bars in common company, strong men walked with handbags, and businessmen closed deals with flickering tongues.

Circles of the Moon

It was the rustling of branches from outside her window that awoke Sarah from a dreamless sleep. The old spruce tree had lived through many storms and stood like a sentinel in the front garden – its heavy limbs swaying under the blanket of air being tossed upon it from the wild churnings of the Atlantic.

Sliding her stuffed turtle tightly beneath her chin, the little girl pictured the waves rushing in great towers towards the shore before crashing down in swirling froth upon the rocks. The sea would gobble mounds of earth back with it to the water and old Ireland would be a much smaller place tomorrow, she supposed, before wondering how close her own house had now gotten to the shoreline. She would need to investigate.

Slipping from the warmth of her bed and placing each foot into a woollen slipper, Sarah quietly tiptoed towards the window – keeping Turtle's furry face close to her cheek for protection. The window was high on the wall, but peaking over its ledge, the girl could just make out the sweeping spectacle which was developing before her eyes.

An electricity pole leaned sideways on the street, allowing its loose wires to flap sporadically against the door of a car. Rubbish bags, leaves, and sections of her father's hedging lay strewn helplessly along the roof of the garden shed. The seafront convulsed in chaos as the sun remained hidden deep beneath the horizon and the moon lingered behind scurrying clouds.

Though Sarah could see the raging white foam spiralling upwards from the promenade, the ocean remained at least a half a mile away; so, it seemed unlikely the house would be swallowed up by the waves for today at least. As she began to thank God for intervening in this matter, Sarah heard the sound of footsteps on the wooden floorboards of the corridor and rushed back beneath her bed covers. The sun was still sleeping beneath the blanket of the sea and she knew it was far too early for little girls to be out their beds. Bringing Turtle back under her chin, she closed her eyes and slowed her breathing to the rhythm of a peaceful dream.

The footsteps continued along the floorboards, growing louder on each step before falling silent on the mat outside her door. Gently, the brass handle creaked as it twisted and a bright shard of light from the corridor snaked along the carpet and up the purple wall of her bedroom. The silence hung momentarily until her father's voice came softly from the open doorway. "Sarah love, I know you're awake."

The girl stretched her arms in a wide arc beneath the blankets. "I'm not awake, Daddy – I was fast asleep and so was Turtle."

"Come on now, Sarah, it's not ok to lie and you know better than that."

"I know – I'm sorry. But it was just that the noise from the wind was so loud I thought the roof would fly off and then the bed would go whooshing out and then the waves would swallow the whole house up."

Her father exhaled and stepped into the room, sitting himself upon the bed so that his warm body nestled into the small of Sarah's back. As he settled on the mattress, a faint scent of fresh aftershave rolled from beneath his dressing gown and tumbled up the bed covers to the little girl's nostrils. It was a pleasant smell which she had come to consistently associate with his presence, and for the first time since she had opened her eyes, Sarah felt safe in the warmth of her sheets.

"You know," her father began, "this house was built by your grandfather nearly fifty years ago. He laid all the blocks and nailed the timber boards that hold up the roof above our heads."

Sarah opened one eye behind Turtle's furry face. "And there's been many circles of the moon since then?"

"Yes, there has," her father replied. "And when he built a house by the sea, he made sure it could stand up to all the water and waves this world could throw its way."

"Grandad built lots of things, didn't he, Daddy?"

"He did, and nothing could be more important to him than a home to protect his own little family. He worked on the house every evening for a year when he was a young man, and he fastened the materials tightly together because he knew the house would need to be strong enough to protect us all. Your uncle James was already running about his feet, and I was in your grandmother's belly waiting to see what the world was like for myself."

"Granny has a soft belly – it must have been lovely and warm in there," Sarah whispered into her pillow.

"Indeed, it was, and Grandad wanted to make sure my new home would be just as cosy as the first one. And so, he wrapped all the pieces of the house together like the blackbird builds his nest outside your window. And just like the blackbirds get the twigs and leaves for their homes from faraway places, your grandad went all over the county to bring back the strongest items he could find."

As she listened to the soft tones of her father's voice drifting over the covers of her bedclothes, Sarah could see her grandfather's white van trundling up the stony passageway towards his new house on the hill. He had the finest materials in the back, and he had been careful to buy them from only the most decent men and women in all of Ireland.

Grandad's face was happy, and his white beard shone with light from the newness of the world. There were no other buildings around the seafront, and the unfinished house glistened above the wide crescent of the bay. His skin was hard, and his hands were strong. They could build houses and protect a family. Yes, she trusted Grandad: when he built something, it was certain to last every rising of the tide and all the circles of the moon.

With each lunar revolution, his voice danced with that of her father's, weaving and trickling through pebbles on the sandy beaches below. It gurgled in bubbles and floated over dark coves and dusty sand dunes until it reached the clifftop and the new home once more.

The old blackbird was building his own house and he smiled dreamily with her grandfather as both bird and man sat on smooth rocks, gazing out over the wonders of the twinkling waves. Content in pleasant company, they slurped mugs of sugary tea and told their tales while the yellow sun tilted his straw hat and shone his smile on the sea.

Someone I Loved in Ireland

We walked about the city in circles once, you and I. Warm footpaths and younger feet. Your toenails were painted a sparkling pink and illuminated the grey footpaths wherever they stood. And when each breeze flowed through your summer dress, I watched it trail behind your slender form and linger in the loose brown strands of your hair.

You would always hold just one of my fingers, hinting that our time together was transient. Neither our hearts nor our fingers could ever truly interlock. Our moments were gloriously finite and embellished with the glow of an imminent end. Where there can be no future, the present must live. I think you told me that.

We strolled that way along the quays and under the shade of Sarsfield Bridge, not knowing where our feet were carrying us. As if discovering the city for the first time together, we wandered through Arthur's Quay Park and watched our shadows spill over the railings and into the river. A ripple rolled against the moss speckled foundations of King John's Castle while our eyes ascended the turret to a red flag fluttering against boundless blue skies.

"The Kingdom of Munster's crimson standard," you assured me with surprising pride, before warmly kissing my lips.

I often looked upon that moment in the years that passed. While turning a pen in my fingers, I would bring the wetness of your lips to mind. The liberty wrought in the impulsive sparks of youth seemed a million miles from my desk in Croydon. Papers strewn. Exams uncorrected. Red pens and unruly students. Constricting ties.

Yet I was glad of the moment. Thankful for the pleasant space it occupied in my mind. I could return to decorate it with my senses whenever the need arose. And as I festooned my happy place with red flags and pink sparkles, it would occur to me that most people had a room of their own. Somewhere to return to.

Now I have returned to you. Back across the waves and touching down in the Shannon marshes. You told me once that the dual carriageway from the airport to the city was the first of its kind in Ireland. That the Americans built it. Transatlantic travel rooted in the region since the flying boats landed in Foynes. Frigid passengers. Irish Coffee. Warm hearts.

Cold hands. As I touch them now in your last repose. Rosary beads wrapped dutifully round your white fingers. Icy passengers on this final journey. Silence. A sunken face still framed in beauty. Peace written softly across each feature. I imagine the lustre of your eyes behind closed lids. The powdered corners of a mischievous smile.

A wedding band marks a union. One more broken heart. My hand met his firm grip as I walked through the door. A kind soul. I want to believe he is a good man. To believe it for you.

How I wish to wake up in yesterday. How we rolled on the grass under the iron bridge in college. Looking down at my face, you noticed I had become distant. Lost beyond the moment. "Where have you gone?" you asked me. I can't remember where. Yet when I gazed upward to your glistening face in the sunlight, a bead of moisture rolling to the tip of your nose, I knew this world had been created just for us. For these moments.

Recalling that moment, I can see the same bead of moisture, but my memories fragment above your head in white clouds of cotton wool. In vain, I reach out so I may spool them to something more permanent. In vain. The memory of your kiss. In vain. Your face now fractured. Your hair in silver bands. Your words: where have you gone?

About the Author

Michael McGrath is an Irish novelist and short story writer who has been published both nationally and internationally in journals such as *Roadside Fiction, Writing Raw, The Ogham Stone* and *Literature Today*. His first novel *The Clock Tower* was released in July 2017.

He works as a second level English teacher and lives in Limerick City, Ireland.

www.michaelmcgrathpen.com

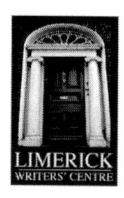

ABOUT THE LIMERICK WRITERS' CENTRE

The Limerick Writers' Centre, based at 12 Barrington Street in Limerick City, is a non-profit organisation established in 2008 and is one of the most active literary organisations in the country. We endeavour to bring ideas about books, literature and writing to as wide an audience as possible, and especially to people who do not feel comfortable in the more traditional arts/literature venues and settings.

At the Centre we share a belief that writing and publishing should be made both available and accessible to all; we encourage everyone to engage actively with the city's literary community. We actively encourage all writers and aspiring writers, including those who write for pleasure, for poetic expression, for healing, for personal growth, for insight or just to inform.

Over the years, we have produced a broad range of writing, including poetry, history, memoir and general prose. Through our readings, workshops and writer groups, our aim is to spread a consciousness of literature. Through public performances we bring together groups of people who value literature, and we provide them with a space for expression.

We are, importantly, also dedicated to publishing short run, high quality produced titles that are accessible to readers.

At our monthly public reading the 'On the Nail' Literary Gathering, we provide an opportunity for those writers to read their work in public and get valuable feedback.

The centre can be contacted through its website: www.limerickwriterscentre.com